Ben's

©2019 by T.Y. Ryan

All rights reserved. No part of this may be reproduced, distributed or transmitted in any form or by any means without prior written permission.

This is a work of fiction. Names, characters, places and incidents are a product of the author's imagination. Any resemblance to actual people, living or dead, or to businesses, events or locales is completely coincidental.

Chapter 1
Chapter 2
Chapter 3
Chapter 4
Chapter 5
Chapter 6
Chapter 7
Chapter 8
Chapter 9
Chapter 10
Chapter 11
Chapter 12
Chapter 13
Chapter 14
Epilogue

Part One

New Mexico

CHAPTER ONE

Ben Moss lifted the red-hot branding iron out of the fire. Satisfied with the bright glow on the business end, he turned to the bellowing calf. His ranch foreman, Edgar Latham, tightened his grip on the struggling animal as its eyes rolled in terror. Latham twisted the rope tighter, using his weight and considerable strength to keep the young steer still. Ben pressed his Lazy Four brand down on the rear haunch. The sizzle of seared flesh was coupled with a wisp of smoke, smelling of burned hair. He held the branding iron still with even pressure for two seconds, then stood back. He saw the mark was crisp and clean, and he gave a short nod. Latham got up, and in the moment it took the angry calf to get to its feet, he had freed the rope. With a final bellow of protest, the calf ran off to join his similarly outraged brothers. They all now bore the sign of Ben's brand—a four lying on its side, next to an F that was also rotated ninety degrees. A day's work done, with the last of the spring calves marked as Ben's property.

"That's the end. Twenty-six," said Latham.

"Not bad for twenty-seven births. Only lost the one."

Latham smiled. "That wolf won't be bothering no more cows. My wife is using his pelt to line a fine winter hat for me."

"Maybe I'll call you Warm Ears from now on." Both men chuckled over this witty exchange. The longest conversation they'd had all day.

They parted. Latham headed for the hogan he had put up in the shade of some cottonwoods by a stream. He was a squat, powerful man. Given the choice, he'd rather be herding sheep. But Ben Moss was a good man to work for. Fair. Just. Maybe because he had once been a lawman, back in Texas. Ben had picked up and moved to New Mexico almost sixteen years back. But the man still had a big helping of Texas in him. Probably why he was so stubborn in his preference for cattle. Texans didn't herd sheep.

Most Texans would never call a Navajo their foreman. But Ben insisted that's what Latham was. Foreman of the ranch. Even if there were no other hands on the payroll, except the drovers they would hire when it was time to take the cows to market at the railhead in Truth Or Consequences, New Mexico. It was only a day's journey, so Latham wasn't foreman of anyone else for long. But he still held himself in higher regard, thanks to his job title. Foreman. It was a title with dignity.

***

As he rode back to his ranch house, Ben sat easy in the saddle. His big Appaloosa, Skip, required no direction from him to get home.

Skip was a big horse; he could ride hard all day and never show it. Ben loved the powerful mount because he reminded him of the horse he'd had back in Texas. Old Hank. He still missed that horse. Best horse that ever carried a man. Even stronger than Skip, if that was possible. Dead six years now. And missed terribly.

Then he gave Skip a pat on the neck. He was a fine horse, near as good a horse as Old Hank. Truth be told, Ben had paid too much for Skip at auction. But this horse had reminded him of Old Hank, with his strong, wide back and powerful bunches of twitching muscle. The resemblance was all it had taken to open Ben's money purse.

He took off his battered Stetson and with his other hand, he pushed back a shock of sweat-dampened graying blond hair away from his deep-set hazel eyes. He lived in a simple ranch house, built of wood he'd cut himself. He lived alone. That was fine with him.

It had been that way ever since he turned his back on Texas and arrived in New Mexico to buy a ranch and start a new life. The scarcity of human contact suited him. He'd seen more human behavior than he ever wanted to see during the eight years he'd served as sheriff of Pendleton, Texas. It was an "unremarkable bump in the road," according to the article printed in the Amarillo Star a couple of weeks after the shootout. That wasn't quite fair, but it was the only spark of truth in the entire piece. Most of it was a pack of lies about "the courageous lawman who took down a murderous gang single-handed with his swift and deadly gun."

It was utter rubbish and brought with it an unwanted notoriety. That wasn't the only reason Ben had quit Texas. But it was sure enough a consideration. Once a man had a reputation as a man who was fast with a gun, it was as good as a target on your back. Every young hot-head with a six-shooter and snoot full of whiskey was a potential challenge. And no matter how many a man might gun down, it would never end until some punk either got lucky or just shot from ambush. No, it wasn't the reason he had left. But it sure had made it easier to pull up stakes.

***

After his familiar dinner of beans and bacon with a slab of soda bread, he lit a lamp and sat down to write a letter back to his sister, Joan Norris. Their regular correspondence comprised the majority of Ben's social interaction. This consisted of semimonthly letters from Joan that kept him far more up-to-date with life in Pendleton,

Texas than he really cared for. Still, he would read every word over and over for weeks, until the next letter arrived. Especially the ones that offered little updates on Cassie Bohn. She was the widow of his best friend, Gary Bohn. Ben followed with interest the occasional scraps about her son. Slade Bohn was nearly sixteen now. He had been shaving for a year already. Ben wished he could see the boy's face. Would it be Gary's? The animated, grinning young man Ben remembered? Were folks just naturally drawn to Slade, the way they had all been charmed by his father, Gary? All folks but one. Harvey Parson. The man who had left Ben's best friend gut shot and dying. Left Gary's body still and lifeless, cooling in the dust.

Ben tried to push the image out of his mind, reading on. But the next thing he read was news that pulled him right back in. Martha Madden, the widow of the killer, Harvey Parson, had passed away. Her son, Davis, who was also Harvey Parson's son, was orphaned now. Davis would go to live with his best friend, Slade Bohn, and his mother, Cassie Bohn. On the very same ranch where Gary had died at the hands of rustlers—the Parson Gang, led by Harvey Parson. Ben shrugged his shoulders, shifting his thoughts back to his sister.

When Ben read her letters, he could hear Joan's voice. He could see the expressions on her face, or how he thought it would be if she were sitting here telling him the stories. But it was Joan's face as a twenty-year-old bride that he saw. Not the thirty-five-year-old woman she'd be now. He'd never seen this older Joan—he wondered if he would even recognize her if he passed her on the street.

Ben's replies to his sister were far more economical. He had no neighbors to bicker with or gossip about. No quilting bees or potluck church dinners to report on. No funerals, no weddings, no newly birthed babies. Tonight, Ben told her how they had gotten the branding done. There wasn't much more to say.

CHAPTER TWO

Arno Parson had been selling stolen cattle to Wells Loomis for over a dozen years. It was always a risky arrangement. Cattle rustlers were as low as horse thieves. And horse thieves, when caught, were subjected to justice at the end of a rope, slung over the nearest tree branch or barn rafter, without anyone bothering with the niceties of a jury trial, or the unnecessary expense of constructing a gallows.

And the rustler's job was a lifetime of hard labor—and a short one at that. There were endless days looking for a vulnerable herd, scouting out an approach and an escape that would give Arno Parson's gang time to rustle the beef. Maybe they'd bother to find a way to change the cow's brand in a convincing way, then drive the rebranded cattle out of the area far enough that they could find a buyer who didn't know—or didn't care—that the cattle were stolen.

Wells Loomis was one who didn't care.

Not that there wasn't plenty of risk on his end, too. But when he dealt with a gang of rustlers, like Arno Parson and his ruffians, it was to his advantage to know the cows were stolen. It gave him an edge and helped him bargain down the price. He knew that by the time the gang had gone to all the trouble to rustle the herd, brand the cows (or not), and drive them to Amarillo, they were going to take the offer Wells Loomis would haggle them into.

By the time the rustlers reached Amarillo, they just wanted to get rid of the stolen property before word could catch up. Sure, if Arno didn't want to take a bad deal, he could take his business elsewhere. But where? Amarillo was a big, busy town, and an awful lot of cows moved through it. So many that it wasn't that hard to mix in a few head of rustled cows, planting them in several different legitimate herds, and shipping them off on the railroad with no one the wiser. If they tried selling stolen beef somewhere with less activity in the cattle market, they would become more visible. The rustlers might get a higher price, or they might get caught. And hanged.

So Arno knew he had to bargain at a disadvantage. Wells Loomis was sharp, and he was treacherous. He wasn't the only game in town. But he was still the best option. He had the right connections; the crooked buyers and middlemen who could take some hot cows from Loomis and never soil their hands by making a direct connection to rustlers like Arno Parson.

Wells Loomis could bring them cattle at a discounted price while offering plausible deniability if anyone got curious about their provenance.

***

It was a rare day for the Texas panhandle, with rain pelting down. The cold wind blew the stinging rain practically sideways as Arno's crew whistled and shouted and snapped the occasional whip, driving a couple dozen trail-beaten steers up a muddy track and into a chute leading to

Wells' corral. Arno sat on his horse, next to Wells, who was, as always, making a personal count of each head and marking down the odd comment on an animal's condition, where it might help him beat the price down even lower.

"Here's another one with them sores on it."

"Ain't sores," Arno lied. "That cow just got hung on some barbed wire. It's nothing."

"Looks to me like a weeping lesion. Hell, could be sick with some kind of cowpox and infect my whole inventory. I don't want that one. Cut it from the herd."

And do what with it? thought Arno. *Bring it back to where we stole it?* Arno shivered as the wind drove freezing, sleety water down his neck. He wanted to get his money, pay off his stooges, and get himself a bottle and plump little woman with a warm, dry bed. "Fine. Give me half price on that one then, you nickel-squeezing tinhorn."

"That's something we better get straight on now."

"What is?"

"The price."

"You know the price. We worked it out last season."

Wells let some air out through his lips, an irritating sound he always made when he was about to gouge you. It was half whistle, half hiss, and neither one really. "Last season was a whole different market, friend."

Arno's hand moved, almost on its own, to the pearl handle of his Colt. He could have this chiseling turd blossom down in the mud and bleeding in the blink of an eye. But then what? His cows were already in the pen. He wasn't about to tell Martinez, his top hand, to get them all out of there and go dragging off with these stinking cows, stashing them someplace while Arno scoured the whole town for another morally deficient buyer. Not in this freezing rain.

He looked sideways at Wells Loomis, who looked warm and comfy in his nice oilskin slicker. He noticed again the special stirrup on the right side of Wells' elegant Mexican-made saddle. It was a perfect custom fit to hold Loomis—Wells' right leg was missing from just below the knee. The Wells-holder was decorated—like the rest of the fine leather saddle—in bright silver Conchos. Probably cost more than the whole herd was worth. Five herds, more like. Just so this skinflint dandy could sit comfortable as you please, and show you how rich he was getting off the sweat of your brow. Arno bit down hard on the hate that boiled up whenever he had dealings with Loomis.

They settled on a price that left Arno seething with anger and shame. Just a little more than seventy cents on the dollar—lower than the bottom-scraping bargain Wells had crammed down his throat last time. He watched Wells open a bulging money purse strapped around his fat belly with another fine-tooled custom leather belt. He snatched the money out of Loomis' hand and turned his horse away without another word.

***

"Slim takings, I'd say," opined Jerry Quincy, as Arno counted out shares to his gang. Quincy was a big, sullen oaf, given to bouts of melancholy. The black moods would build and build, his face getting more grim, his eyes darker, the curl of his lip becoming a snarl. Then he'd just vanish on his own for a day, a week, or whatever he felt like. When he came back, his black mood would have lifted some. When this happened, Arno knew that wherever they were at the time, they better ride on without delay. Because before long, someone would discover a body—usually a woman, sometimes just a girl—and the locals would start looking for the monster who'd inflicted this outrage on them.

"You want to register a complaint, Quincy?"

The big brute looked Arno in the eye for a moment. And then he huffed out a sound that might pass for a laugh. And he backed down. "Just saying. Ain't your fault, boss. Nobody saying that."

"It's that one-legged sidewinder Loomis," Martinez ventured. Quincy and the four other lowlife desperados seated around the table grunted in agreement. Every man among them was an unredeemable sociopath, with filth under his nails, and blood on his hands.

Red Calby was a one-eyed knuckle-dragger with a taste for unnatural acts on unwary women.

Sammy Yost was wanted in Saint Louis for the unsolved disappearance of his sister, who had been a month or so from delivering a child. His, was the general opinion.

Vern Ebersky had been a butcher back in Krakow. So he said. He had sailed for America five years ago, just around the time when the authorities started asking questions about what, exactly, Ebersky put into the sausages he pedaled. Questions that neighbors began to ask when the population of local cats and dogs went into a steady decline.

And then there was Gandy. Just Gandy. Nobody was sure if Gandy could actually speak. If so, no one could remember ever hearing him say anything. He was a small, wiry man who might not look like much. People tended not to notice him. When they did, it was usually too late.

One moment, he was a still shape, off to the side of a man's peripheral vision. Then in the next instant, that man would be holding a bloody rope of intestines in his hands, his belly slashed open quicker than a blink. Gandy was lightning fast with every one of the half-dozen knives he stashed on his person. He had a stiletto in his boot, a straight razor in his hip pocket, a switchblade inside his vest, on the right side. On the left side, he kept a folding utility knife, honed to a deadly edge. The Bowie knife in the sheath strapped to his leg was almost as long as his thigh. And the sixth knife? Nobody knew where he kept that one. But it was there—somewhere. No doubt about that.

When Arno had finished distributing the paltry take from Wells Loomis, he pushed away from the table. He got a bottle from the bar and climbed the stairs to find himself some female company. The thing nagging at him was that he had to think about how much he could afford. That wasn't right.

He tried to focus on taking his pleasure with the whore. But he kept worrying about how little he would have left in his pocket. He could not get past his anger at Wells Loomis or his shame at being bested by him. It bothered him so much that he could not get his money's worth with his soiled dove. That put him into a darkening fury. It just wasn't right. Something had to be done.

***

Wells Loomis had a lot of business to finish. He had passed around the green to grease the wheels with the men at the stock auction. He had slipped the usual envelope to the shipping manager with the railroad. He had collected his 'percentage' from the nine saloons/brothels in which he held a silent partnership. He still had bribes to pay the mayor, the sheriff and his deputies, and the railroad detective. He would have to hit the bank in the morning, to deposit some of the cash weighing him down. But tonight, he would stash it in the safe in his home office.

He rode his horse directly into the carriage house behind his two-story, six-bedroom brick mansion. There was a lantern lit, and he called out for Jefferson, the stable hand who lived up in the hayloft, and was expected to be available day or night. There was no answer. Fury boiled up inside him. He was bone tired. Hungry. And he needed a hand to get down off his horse.

"Jefferson! Get your ass over here, you lazy—" The rest of his words caught in his throat when he noticed a pool of blood which was seeping out below the gate of one of the horse stalls. He felt a rising panic as he moved the horse closer. When he saw his man, Jefferson, lying dead, throat cut ear to ear, he tried to wheel his horse around. He wanted to dash out of the carriage house—but as he turned the animal, he heard the humming noise of a rope whipping the air. The lariat was thrown perfectly and in an instant, it was around him, pinning his arms to his sides, squeezing tight as a python. The horse bolted, but the rope held Wells Loomis and yanked him off. He was dangling in the air now, hanging three feet off the ground, kicking helplessly with his one good leg.

As Arno stepped out into the light, he wet himself. "Listen, Arno. Let's talk about this …"

"Negotiation time is over," Arno growled. He turned and spoke to someone in the shadows. "Gandy? Let me see that Arkansas Toothpick you've got there. I need to carve out a new arrangement."

CHAPTER THREE

The next day, Ben rode into town with his reply letter, to mail it back to Joan. There was no hurry. There was nothing in the letter that mattered. But as Skip carried him along the trail to Truth or Consequences, he thought about Slade Bohn. And it made him think about Gary …

Gary came west from Tennessee. He'd fought for the rebels, but when he mustered out, he saw no future for himself in the Old South. It had been a stupid war.

But Texas? Sure, it was another defeated Rebel state. But Texas wasn't beaten. It was booming. And by God, it was huge. With plenty left for the taking. Its massive gravity drew in everything—

Cherokee from Mississippi, German farmers, English Lords, Norwegian sodbusters. There were also the cattle punchers, Comanches, Italians, Polish, Mexicans, and Irishmen along with Chinese workers for railroads. Texas was another fertile American melting pot, stirring with pioneer grit and a thousand purposes.

Besides, Gary told anyone who listened, if Texas was good enough to pull Davey Crockett out of Tennessee, then it was good enough for him. And he arrived with a good deal more than forty acres and a mule. His older brother, William, had been a successful lawyer, and a shrewd man. Shrewd enough to keep some of his money in Yankee banks, and even one in Canada. His brother was a patriotic son of the South, though. And he was single. So William raised up a company of men with his own money and made himself a colonel. He wasn't a very good colonel, though. He stopped a musket ball with his head at Shiloh.

When Gary got back from the war, he found he had inherited a decent-sized estate. Not a fortune, but plenty enough for a man to start a new life in a new world.

Gary had bought a good-sized cattle ranch just outside Pendleton. But unlike Ben, Gary was a people person—outgoing, open, and friendly. He had a marvelous sense of humor, the kind which was never cruel. He could swap stories with any man, flirt with any woman, and never make anybody mad. He had an infectious grin, and his laugh was downright contagious.

His whole personality was the opposite of Ben, the taciturn, serious young fellow recently elected sheriff in Pendleton. So of course, Gary and Ben became the best of friends.

There was a girl, Cassie Markley, who Ben started to court. She was lively, smart, and not at all hard on the eyes. She and Ben found each other attractive. They started to keep company—but it was not meant to be. First off, he was so quiet she felt awkward around him, and that made him even more reserved. But most of all, she was afraid. Not of him; he seemed gentle and could be so kind to anyone. But she was afraid of the danger his job put him in, day and night. Pendleton was definitely what folks called a cow town. It had a bank, a gunsmith, an express office for mail and stagecoaches, a mercantile store, a train station, a tailor, a school, two churches … and seven saloons. Being a railroad stop, a lot of cattle came through town. And when the cowboys drove them to the railroad, it was the end of their trail, and they got paid.

Then they got drunk. What they didn't drink up, they spent on loose women or lost at cards to quick-handed gamblers. There were fights to bust up every night. There was regular gunplay—usually just noisy, aggressive foolishness. But even that led to the odd murder or maiming.

One night, for the third time in a month, Ben broke a date with Cassie at the last minute. A big cattle drive had shown up. The town was going to get crazy that night. He said he had to stay on duty. Cassie said he was strong and brave and wonderful, and this thing with them was never going to work out. She could not stand the uncertainty of his life.

The next day, Gary saw his friend with a black eye and a long face. The eye was from a brawl in a saloon he had tried to prevent. The long face was also related to the brawl, in that it was one of the reasons Cassie broke it off with him.

"But, Ben, I know you have feelings for her. Don't you?" Gary had asked.

He had shrugged, then nodded.

"Well, then, the thing to do is talk it out with her. Let her know how you feel about her—have you even said that to her?"

"Not in … so many words."

"That just never works, Ben. Women love feelings. They even like to talk about them. Know what I mean?"

"Sure. Well, not exactly."

"You just need to listen to her worries. Let her know you understand her concern. Tell her you'll always be careful because she means so much to you."

Ben looked at the dust. Moved it a little with the toe of his boot. Then he looked up at Gary, and said, "Can you tell her?"

"Tell her what?"

"You know. What you said."

"Thunderation, son. That's never going to work. Not in a million years. It has to be you. That's the whole point."

Ben nodded. He worked his tongue around in his mouth. Spat into the dusty road. Dragged his boot over the spittle, burying it in the dust. "So?" he said. "Can you tell her for me?"

Gary gave him a light, friendly punch on the shoulder.

"All right. I'll talk to her."

Cassie and Gary were married six months later. Ben was his best man. Whenever he saw how happy they were together, he felt not jealousy, but relief.

When he looked back at those times now, he could see the bitter irony of what had happened. Cassie had married a joyful, garrulous, stable man, instead of a sheriff in constant danger, surrounded by frequent, explosive violence. But it was Gary, an amiable, gentle, forbearing soul without an angry bone in his body, who had gotten himself shot by the Parson Gang. Gary who had ended up making Cassie a widow.

***

Ben nodded to Tom Remley, the express clerk, as he came in. He walked up to the counter, giving a wave with his letter to Joan. "Got a reply here to that letter from my sister."

"That was quick. You two are pretty chatty on paper."

"That's how you'll get rich, Tom. Selling stamps."

"That's a good one," Tom said. Though it wasn't. But getting a dozen words out of Ben Moss was a challenge, and he loved a challenge. Then he played his next card. "By the way," he said, pulling a letter from the sorting cabinet behind the counter, "You got another one here already." And he handed over the new letter to Ben with a flourish. "You're becoming a man of letters." When this bon mot fell flat, he added, "Get it? Man of letters, because you got another …"

Tom stopped as he was not getting a laugh. He knew he wasn't going to. There was a look of dread on Ben's face. "Something wrong, Ben?"

"That's what I'm thinking." Ben stared at the letter with foreboding.

"Oh, don't say that. You ain't even opened it. Why would you say a thing like that?"

"Why would she write me another letter just two days after she mailed the last one?"

"Well … er, I don't know. Don't ask me. Just read the thing."

Ben nodded and walked out of the express office, holding the letter like it was what he feared it would be. A death notice.

***

Ben walked up to the bar in the Hatfield Tavern. Mick Hatfield knew him by sight only. Ben rarely went into any saloon. He wasn't much of a drinker, but that wasn't it. In his experience, nothing good happened in saloons.

"Whiskey?"

Ben was staring at the letter, set on the bar in front of him. He nodded, "Double."

Hatfield slapped a glass down in front of Ben and gave him a very generous pour. Almost to the brim. As Ben looked up at him, Hatfield smiled. "Looks like you need it, pal."

Ben took a big gulp. It burned down through him. He picked up the letter, then put it down and took another deep drink.

Ben sat on his barstool. When he had finished the glass, Hatfield poured another without being asked. Ben reached for it—and then stopped. Instead, he took a deep breath and broke the seal on the envelope.

CHAPTER FOUR

Cassie Bohn nudged her best friend, Joan Norris, and then handed her a handkerchief. "She's gone too soon," Cassie said, hoping to comfort her weeping friend.

Joan dabbed at her eyes, watching the casket being lowered into the earth. "I can't help it. That poor, poor boy. An orphan now." They both watch as Davis Madden, the son of the dead woman in the casket, sobbed loudly and openly. He was a tall, brawny youth of seventeen.

"Martha was so proud of Davis," said Cassie. "She raised such a fine young man."

"Nothing like that father of his," said Joan.

"Harvey Parson got just what he deserved," sniffed Cassie.

"Thanks to your brother Ben, he did."

"And look what it cost him," Joan answered. Then she looked at her friend Cassie, and added quickly, "Not that his leaving was anything compared to what you've been through."

Cassie could tell Joan was worried she had hurt her feelings. "That's all right," she told her friend. "I understand what you meant. Harvey Parson was a black stain on this town. He killed my Gary, but he also hurt nearly everyone in this town, one way or another. And I know how hard it was for you, Ben leaving after all that business."

Joan nodded but still tried to console her lifelong best friend. "Still, that's all nothing, compared to what it cost you. And Slade. Parson robbed you of a husband, and your son of a father." Joan dabbed at her eyes again. "At least Ben is still alive. And I can still trade letters with him."

"I miss Ben, too," Cassie said, with a deeper sadness than Joan expected. Then Cassie tried to lighten her tone. "He was always a good man. I'm glad you can keep in touch with him. How is he?"

Joan almost laughed. "Can anybody ever tell with him? Remember the way he'd answer a question with a shrug? Rub his foot in the dirt, as if he could dig up the answer?"

"Sure do. Real well," Cassie said. "But Ben was always a kind soul. Even if he didn't talk about it. There was more inside him than what he could show."

"Well, he was never easy to talk to, so just imagine how quiet he can be on paper. I swear, one day I expect I'll open one of his letters, and all it will say is "Yep … Nope … Maybe … Uh-huh … Could be. Then a drawing of Ben shrugging his shoulders."

They both smiled at that. They didn't laugh, but they did both stop crying and smiled at each other with the memory.

Then Joan looked over at Davis and saw how Cassie's son, Slade, supported his weeping friend, his arm going around the bigger boy. "I'm glad Davis has your boy for a friend. He's got a good heart, too, your son."

"Thank you, Joan."

"And it's all to your credit. You're a remarkably strong woman."

Cassie heard this all the time. If a man ran his ranch and raised a son, people would say he was doing his duty. But somehow if a woman did it, that required a whole testimonial. "A lot of life is just doing what you don't have a choice about," Cassie said to Joan. "Raise a child, run a ranch, bury a husband. You just have to do what's called for, no matter if it hurts or it don't. But it hurts less if you just get on with it."

"I'm not just talking about the doing. You're strong inside. Even when folks around here snubbed Martha because her husband was a lowdown snake, you didn't. You made a friend of her."

"That wasn't something I set out to do. Just sort of happened. Due to the boys, I guess. They've always been like, well, brothers almost."

"They had a lot in common," Joan said. "Growing up with no father around."

"And I had so much in common with Martha. We just understood each other."

"Well, I will never understand what Martha ever saw in that scum she married. Harvey Parson was a bad, bad man."

"Martha knew that. But she didn't want to know it. And you remember, when he first turned up, Harvey seemed like nothing worse than a charming rogue. He swore up and down to Martha his thieving days were all in the past."

"And she believed that? Even when he'd ride off with those filthy saddle tramps hanging around with his brother for weeks on end? What was wrong with that woman, falling for him?"

"What was wrong? Well, let's see. She was a twenty-eight-year-old spinster …"

"Thornback, you mean," said Joan, cutting in.

"Beg your pardon?"

"Well. An unmarried woman becomes a spinster when she turns twenty-four without finding a man. But when she turns twenty-six and still hasn't married, the correct term is a thornback."

"Joan, you always had a way with words, so I don't dispute you on your terms. But spinster, thornback, whatever people want to call it, it doesn't make life any easier for a woman."

"No. I reckon not."

"And it was lucky Martha had that money her father left her or I don't think a single man would have showed her any interest at all."

"Do you think she knew Harvey just married her for the money?"

"Martha was a plain-looking woman. But not stupid."

The two women quieted now, as the preacher began saying his bit. Cassie noticed now there was a stranger standing near Reverend Allrich. He was freshly shaven, with a new-looking haircut, his well-oiled hair neatly parted down the middle. His fine suit of clothes appeared to be both expensive and newly purchased. Even his shiny shoes.

She also noticed the man didn't seem to hear a word that the reverend was saying. His attention was on the boys, Davis and Slade. Joan noticed this too and thought to herself that something about him seemed off. She was about to whisper a comment to her friend, but Cassie spoke first. "See that fellow? Over near the preacher?"

"I see him, all right."

"Well, I saw him first." Cassie kept a solemn look on her face. But she was clearly biting down on a smile. "That's about the fanciest set of duds I've seen in this town, ever. Cuts quite the figure, I'd say."

"Cassie," Joan whispered. "You're a scandal, you are."

"Really, Joan? Thought you said what I am is a thornback." And Cassie couldn't help letting a tiny giggle escape.

Joan's face flared crimson. "Cassie, I swear …" But she didn't finish what it was she wanted to take an oath about. About this, even Joan was at a loss of words for once.

***

The dapper stranger stood off to the side as one by one, the mourners walked by the grieving Davis Madden. The boy did his best to give a respectful thank-you to each one. But it got harder with every handshake. By the time the crowd had finally dispersed, he stood with only his friend Slade at his side. Davis sniffed again, trying to hold back the urge to throw himself down on his mother's grave and cry for a year.

"Don't worry about none of them," Slade said. "You can cry all you want to, and I'll take a brick bat to anybody who says 'boo' about it."

"You're the best friend I have," Davis said, after a moment.

"Same. Anything I can do …"

"Could you just …" Before he could finish, Davis choked up.

"How about I just leave you here?" Slade said softly. "I can see you later. Okay?"

With a sniff, Davis nodded once. Slade threw his arms around his friend and gave him a rough version of a hug. "Mom's cooking up a fat hen. She expects you for dinner before sundown." Then he slipped away, leaving Davis alone by the grave.

***

The stranger pulled at the tight collar of his starched white shirt. His new clothes had cost a good piece of money. Not that he couldn't afford it. He still had over six hundred dollars in his pockets. And he looked forward to the prospect for a lot more.

But first, what he needed was a good drink, or three.

The man paid for a whole bottle and moved across the saloon. He sat himself down at an empty table, not far from a gambler who was separating fools from money, as God meant him to do. The man shook his head. *Idiot cowpunchers. Suckers. The town was full of them. Still.*

"Excuse me, sir." The stranger looked up at the Right Reverend Joe Allrich. "I don't mean to intrude. But I noticed you today, at the service for Martha Madden."

"Noticed you too, Father."

"Father? Oh dear, no. That's an honorific reserved for the Papists." He put out his hand and as the stranger shook it, he added, "My title is that of reverend. Joe Allrich, sir. Welcome to Pendleton, Texas."

"Long," said the stranger. "Perry Long."

"Pleasure, Mr. Long."

"Thank you, Reverend. I would ask you to sit and have a drink, but with your, uh … your calling? I suspect you would politely decline."

"Hate the sin, sir ..." said Allrich, as he swept an empty, unwashed glass off another table, "... but love the sinner."

He pulled out a chair and placed his glass in a handy spot to have it filled. The stranger uncorked his whiskey bottle and poured. "Thank you, good traveler," the preacher said, lifting a glass and holding it for a toast. Perry Long raised his own glass. "The mystery of God's creation," said Allrich, and took the glass at a swallow.

Perry smiled at this malleable man of the cloth. "Amen, sir," he said, and just as he was about to take a drink, he added, "Live and let live."

Perry poured and listened, listened and poured. Reverend Allrich knew just about everything there was to know about Pendleton and the folks who lived there. He was never a shy man. But the more he drank, the more he unveiled. And Perry Long meant to pick him clean.

The preacher told Perry all about the late Martha Madden. Madden was her given name. She had taken the name of the fellow she had married, Harvey Parson, but he'd turned out to be … "a man at frequent odds with the law." After begetting a child, Davis, Harvey had gotten himself killed in a shootout with the sheriff. So Martha had been left with a baby to care for on her own. She'd dropped the name of this outlaw and taken up her maiden name of Madden again.

"And this lawman who shot the outlaw? He still around?"

"No, sir. He moved on, soon after. Somewhere west, I believe. Arizona, perhaps."

"Or New Mexico?"

"Couldn't say. But the sheriff had plenty of reason to shoot that rascal. It turned out the man was wanted in six other states for robbery, rustling, and murder. Had a whole gang, but made sure they kept away from Pendleton. He wanted to live a respectable life here. And comfortable, thanks to Martha. She had quite a sum put away, from some inheritance, if I'm not mistaken."

"I see. I suppose it will all go to the boy?"

"Well, I can't say anything about that. There's a circuit judge who'll ride through next week. He'll be reading the will and such."

"Hmmm …" Perry nodded. He refilled the glass in front of Allrich. "Was she ill for a long time? Martha, I mean."

"She was determined to see her boy go off to college back east. That's what kept her going for so long. Oh, those last two months, she suffered the tortures of the damned."

"Left the son well set up, though, is that right?"

"With money, yes. But from what I know, there's no other family."

"Well, it sounds like you know the family well."

"Fairly well. Especially toward the end. I often sat with Martha and prayed for her. Tried to be a comfort."

"Surprised she didn't ask you to become guardian for the boy."

"Me?" The idea almost seemed to shock the reverend. "Oh, no, no. That wouldn't have been good, not at all. Besides, the boy was already set to stay with another family. His best friend's family. Slade Bohn. Mrs. Bohn, Cassie by name. She's a widow. But she runs their ranch as well as any man could do. Martha named her guardian, in fact …" Allrich paused. "I shouldn't be talking about this. But it's all in the will."

"Sounds like you know that will pretty good."

"I haven't seen the document."

"But she told you about it. Martha?" Perry topped off the whiskey glass. Allrich took another drink. Perry waited him out. He knew this fellow was the kind of drunk who couldn't keep his trap shut.

Finally, patience paid off. "Well … I'm not one to speak out of school."

"Of course not. But I can tell folks trust you."

"Trust. Right you are. A trust."

"She put the money in a trust for the boy."

The preacher tried to look subtle as he nodded. "Until he's twenty-one. And Cassie's just the right person to be trustee."

"Who's Cassie?"

"Cassie Bohn. I told you. Davis, he's going to stay with Cassie and her son Slade. Didn't I?

"Yes, yes. The widow rancher, you said."

"You see, Martha had no living relatives. Unless one should come forward to challenge the will. But that's hardly likely, I'd say."

They drank for another hour. Long pried out every last secret and scrap of gossip about the entire town. When the bottle was empty, they were the very best of friends. The reverend even invited Mr. Long back to his rooms, where there happened to be at least half a bottle of rum they might sample next.

Perry had to help the good reverend keep his feet as they headed for the boarding house where Allrich lived. Going up the front steps, the reverend stumbled, and Perry just barely managed to catch him before he fell on his face.

"No offense, Padre, but you're looking a bit under the weather."

"I'm feeling a bit dizzy. Believe I missed lunch."

"Be a shame if folks saw you in this condition. Is there another way, so we don't have to go through the parlor?"

"Sir, you're correct. Quite right. Let's employ the back stairs. Free of prying eyes and wagging tongues."

Practically carrying the potted preacher, Perry steered him around back and up a set of outside stairs. There was a door up on the second story landing at the top. It took a lot of effort to get the drunken man up to the top of the wooden steps. By the time they reached the landing, Allrich had gone beyond looking green at the gills. The reverend's cheeks puffed up and there was no holding back. He vomited explosively over the railing.

"Oh my … that's terribly embarrassing." The preacher noticed a significant dribble of puke on his shirt and suit coat. "What a mess I appear."

"You do, sir," said Perry. "You drink too much. And you talk too much."

Allrich tried to focus bleary eyes on his companion. "Thank you, sir. I'm feeling better now that the poison is purged." He plunged his hand into various pockets, patting himself for a key to open the door.

"Got to watch your step. You could take a nasty fall," said Perry.

Allrich held his key up proudly. "Aha. Got it. Shall we adjourn to my room for a sociable refreshment?"

"I think you've had enough," said Perry. He put his hands on either side of the preacher's head. It almost looked like a gesture of affection.

Then he wrenched Allrich's head with a violent twist. There was a brief second of shock and pain on the preacher's face as he heard the sound of the crack! His fourth and fifth cervical vertebrae snapped.

He was already dead when Perry let him drop, tumbling over and over as he banged and smashed down to the bottom of the stairs.

"Sorry, Padre," said Perry, as he passed the body. "But like I said. You drink too much. And you talk too much." Perry Long turned down the alley behind the boarding house, and walked away …

When he reached the street, Perry walked back toward the saloon. But then, across the street, he saw the Madden boy, Davis, trudging down from the ceremony. His tears were dry now, although there were grimy streaks of dust showing the trail they had taken when they rolled down his cheeks. Again, Perry was struck by the familiar look of the boy's face. He crossed the street, his course intersecting with Davis Madden. As the boy looked up at him, he tipped his hat and said with solemnity, "Good day, son. I'm so sorry for your loss."

"Thank you, sir." He looked closer at the man. "I noticed you at Mother's service." He gestured at the man's attire. "Hard to miss, in these parts."

"Respect, Davis. It always pays to show respect."

"Sir? How is it you know my name?"

"I regret I did not introduce myself earlier, but it did not seem proper at the cemetery. But allow me," said the stranger, and he produced a calling card. As he handed it over to Davis, he also said his name: "I am Perry Long."

"Did you know my ma?"

"That I did, son. As children. She was, in fact, my cousin."

"What? Ma said she didn't have any living relatives."

"That may be due to a mistaken report that I was lost at sea. This was years and years ago. It was only recently I learned she had moved to Texas." Perry Long heaved a mournful sigh. "I'm simply heartbroken I didn't get here before …" Then he smiled at the boy, putting a hand on his shoulder. "But excuse me, talking of myself. It is nothing, compared to your own loss."

"But if you're her cousin, aren't you my … is it second cousin?"

"Not exactly. If Martha is my first cousin, it makes you my first cousin, once removed."

"Removed from what?"

"Good question. I don't know. From my generation, maybe?"

"So, is that what I call you?"

"Fortunately, no. The correct term of address would simply be 'Uncle.' I am your Uncle Perry. And I will call you my nephew. How is that?"

Davis didn't quite know how to answer. "I guess …"

"Fine. Now then. How about if your Uncle Perry buys you a fine dinner?"

"Tonight?"

"I am planning to eat tonight, yes. You?"

"Sure. I mean, I am eating. But at Slade's house. I'm staying with them. Have been for the past couple months, with Ma so sick and all."

"Slade? Is he the boy with you today?"

"Yes, sir. But you know what? His mom? She's a really great cook. And I know she wouldn't mind setting an extra place. Especially to meet my new uncle."

***

Cassie was about to take the chicken out of the oven when she glanced out the window. Two horses were approaching. One was carrying Davis Madden, she could tell even at this distance. The other, though? As they got closer, she could see the clothes—the same ones she and Joan had remarked on at the cemetery. What on earth was Mr. Fancy Pants doing there?

Riding up into the yard, Arno Parson looked around at the familiar setting. This was the place where it had all started. Nearly sixteen years, it had been. His damn brother, Harvey, taking on airs when he'd married that bitch. And sired this wet nose riding with him. The kid did look like his brother, Harvey, though. No doubt about that. The boy bore a family resemblance to Arno, too. That was good. It would help with his plans.

Arno started to blame himself. Arno was the one who had decided to rustle some cattle from this ranch here. What the hell else was he supposed to do, though? The gang was falling apart. They were broke. They were bored. And they took it as an insult that Harvey had told them to stay the hell out of town. Told them not to steal anything in the whole damn county. They could all starve, just because Harvey didn't want any trouble in his fat, comfortable life. The gang wasn't good enough to show their faces in Pendleton, Texas. His own brother, Arno himself, unwelcome. And since that kid of his was born, Harvey had only gotten worse. Giving one excuse after another why it wasn't a 'good time' to pull a job. That was no kind of leadership.

Oh, Arno understood Harvey's reasons just fine. If the gang had started to operate in this territory, it most likely would have come back on Harvey. And the more he thought about it, the more that seemed like a good idea. Rob one of these local sodbusters, and Harvey would have no choice but to get out of town. He'd return to the gang full-time. All to get back to doing what they do—rustling cattle. The way Arno saw it, that would be doing Harvey a favor.

It had started out okay. The woman, that would be this Cassie, he thought, was alone when they all rode in. She'd been a ripe thing. And his boys had spent too long on the trail without any. Arno had made a couple of comments, pretty clever as he recalled. But before he could dismount and mount—that was it, he remembered—Jack Witter had already hopped off his horse and was moving in.

"Hold your horses, sonny," he told Arno. "I'm taking the first slice of this cherry pie, and you can have sloppy …" They were all surprised when the woman pulled a Colt Peacemaker from some fold in her skirt.

Jack stopped for a second. "Well, well. I like 'em with a little spirit in 'em." Jack got only one step closer before the woman put a bullet in his thigh, just above the kneecap. Two of the gang pulled pistols of their own.

That was when the man opened fire from the barn. The husband. Good shot, too. He killed Maxwell's pinto right out from under him and broke Maxwell's arm when the horse rolled on him. Arno and the gang were all scrambling to find cover, firing away, wild shots flying all over but hitting nothing.

The woman made it back into the house and now was taking potshots at them with a shotgun whenever they tried to stick a head up. Now she and her man had them caught in a crossfire.

The ranch was not quite a mile outside Pendleton. That must be how someone heard all the shooting. Next thing Arno knew, a horse was coming. Harvey jumped off his mount and dived behind the barrels where Arno was hiding. Arno got three words out before Harvey had his gun out. But instead of firing at the man in the barn, Harvey whopped Arno across the face with the barrel. Arno wanted to fight back, but he knew Harvey would beat him easily. So he curled up and tried to dodge as Harvey gave him a pistol whipping.

And then it all went straight to hell.

***

He pushed those old memories aside when Cassie stepped outside to greet Davis, her new ward, and he introduced the dapper man with him as his Uncle Perry. She spent half a second looking him over, as if she was finding something wrong with the picture. Arno remembered the gun. Was she packing under those skirts again?

But Arno was confident she would not recognize him. He'd never been closer than twenty yards from her. And he'd been only nineteen or twenty then. He'd been dressed in clothes made filthy from living hard outside. Plus, back then, his black hair had fallen down below his shoulders, and half his face had been buried behind a thick, bushy beard. But look at him now. Clean-shaven, slick haircut, and dressed sharper than a Natchez riverboat gambler on a long win streak. He was Perry Long; Arno Parson felt invisible to her.

"Mr. Long, is it?"

"Yes, ma'am," he said. And to himself he noted this woman was still a fine looker indeed. That was a plus. So when Cassie invited Perry Long inside, asking if he would share supper with them, he gave her his most winning smile.

***

After he left the ranch, Arno rode straight to the arroyo where Martinez was keeping the rest of the gang out of sight. As Perry Long, Arno had done his best charming act on this Cassie woman. He'd never mentioned a word about the trust. That would be rushing things. No, he'd decided he should get closer first. A lot closer.

He spelled out a plan for his bushwhacking minions.

And they listened to him. Because, Arno thought, they believed in him. Respected him. He was their leader. A real leader. Not like Harvey. The murderous half-wits of that old Parson Gang were gone. Not a single man was left alive. Those men who had raided the Bohn Ranch almost sixteen years ago were all as dead as Harvey now. Shot. Hanged. Stabbed. Purged.

This was a new Parson Gang. Arno's gang. And not a man of Arno's had ever known Harvey. The days of standing in his brother's shadow had been over for a long, long time. Almost every slight, every hurt, every humiliation he had suffered under his brother had been erased. Almost …

There were just a few loose ends to tie up. Then he could finally put those black old days to rest forever.

CHAPTER FIVE

After the flour, bacon, molasses, coffee, and salt were squared away on the buckboard for the short but bumpy ride back out to the ranch, Cassie made sure the nails and roll of barbed wire were also secured. She was just about to get going, when the window of the mercantile store caught her eye. Specifically, that jar of jawbreakers. And the rock candy.

She smiled to herself. Slade and Davis were both nearly grown men—in size. But they were still boys. And candy would always be candy. She went in to obtain a supply of rewards, bribes, and temptations is sugary form. Even if they were too big to spank, there were still ways to control those two. And the surefire best was still candy.

She was shocked when she came back out with a sack of sweets and saw two men—saddle tramp ruffians, by the look of them—pawing through her freshly purchased goods. The bigger one, who was both taller and quite heavy, had unwrapped a side of bacon and was sniffing at it with a critical expression.

"Yeeech! Too much sol," opined Vern Ebersky, and to be certain, he actually put his gross, furry tongue on the meat and licked it.

"Speak English, you stupid …" Gandy said, remarkably gruff to a man who towered over him and outweighed him by half a ton or so.

"Salt, you ignorant runt," replied the former butcher of Krakow. "These peasants have no idea how to cure meat properly."

"Lemme see," Gandy said, and a glittering blade appeared in his hand. With the slightest flick, the blade peeled off a hunk from the bacon. Gandy chewed, evaluating. "It's pretty damn tasty, you ask me. Want a slice?"

"Want to have a couple of fingers shot off?" Cassie said in a flat, even voice, punctuated by the sound of a Colt Peacemaker being cocked.

Gandy was just about to give the woman some lip in return. But her arm was awful steady. He'd seen a number of women point a gun before. This was the first time he'd seen one whose hands didn't shake. And she obviously know where to point it.

But what Cassie did not count on was the sudden move from behind as Sammy Yost struck her arm, knocking the Colt down in the dust. She tried to rake his face with her nails as her boot heel crushed down on his instep. But as she dragged her fingernails across Sammy's cheek, Red Calby left the spot where he'd been leaning on a hitching post and grabbed Cassie's arms, pinning them against her. She threw her head back, and her skull cracked his nose with a sound they all could hear. Red staggered back, blood streaming from his broken nose. Cassie stooped down to grab her gun, but Gandy kicked it away.

"Hey, Red," Gandy teased Calby as the blood ran down his face, "we were just discussing the taste of bacon in these parts." He nodded to the side of meat Ebersky was still holding. "Wanna take a sniff?"

This was about as droll a punch line as any of them would ever come up with. It was received with howls and hoots of mirth. Infuriated, Red Calby lost his cool. His fist shot out. He only struck Cassie a glancing blow because she was quick to duck the full impact.

Still, the pain rocked her. She realized that four trail bums were now surrounding her on four sides. "Get away from my stuff," she said sharply, struggling to keep the fear out of her voice. She could feel a throbbing sting where the knuckles had bruised her cheek. Her eyes swept the faces of her assailants. She could almost smell the excitement the violence kindled in these men.

She realized this was only going to escalate. She wheeled on the closest, Sammy

Yost, and hammered him across the face with the sack full of jawbreakers. The bag exploded, scattering a shower of candy that caused another gale of laughter from the crew of thugs. She used this distraction to kick Vern Ebersky right in his tender bits, shoving past him and breaking into a run.

She dashed into the street. But that's when she saw another one of those apes approaching from across the street, blocking her escape. Jerry Quincy made these other desperados look like a troupe of Christmas carolers. Grime crusted his leering face, and his grotesque smile showed teeth as black as his greasy hair and wild, bristly beard. Quincy lunged, but she cut left, breaking clear of the brute.

But Gandy was already on her from behind, fast as a mongoose. She screamed now. But it did nothing to slow down the five men now closing around her in a tighter circle. They began shoving her, tossing her from one to the other, pawing at her body. As soon as she tried to push one set of grasping fingers off her, she was passed along to the next, who caught her, and explored her with another molesting grasp. She heard cloth rip as her sleeve was torn apart and bared her shoulder. This set the pack of dogs growling, as the sight of bare skin fueled their cruel lust.

"Let's see some more," she heard one of the morons blurt. She heard another rip. Somebody pinned her arms now, and she could feel hands crawl all over her as they pressed in close. She bucked and kicked and spit, she tried to break free. But she knew she didn't stand a chance. They were moving Cassie boldly now, dragging her away from the public street. She fought even harder now, as she was pulled helpless toward an alley. She knew if they got her out of the street, they could enjoy themselves with some privacy. This was happening. The truth of it struck her like a carpet beater.

Then she heard the gunshot—BLAM! The hands holding her let go, as someone shouted. "Next man to touch this woman is gonna lose a body part, and I ain't talking about a toe."

Sammy Yost started to let his hand drift toward the hog's leg in his holster. Then suddenly, Yost was lying on the street, holding the tooth that the blow from a pistol barrel had just knocked from his jaw.

"Anyone else have an opinion you want to share?" He left them a second to consider this, then fired again, kicking up dirt and stones at Gandy's feet. He turned and ran. The others wasted no time following, and they scattered in all directions.

"Are you injured, Mrs. Bohn?"

Cassie looked up, brushing a tear from her eye. Before her, looking as gallant as he was dapper, stood Perry Long.

***

After reading through Joan's description of the assault against Cassie, Ben was so overcome with fury he nearly jumped off the barstool. He wanted to hop on Skip and beat hooves for Texas right then.

But Ben had trained himself never to seek blood in anger. It would either get you killed, or get you hanged for murder. Still, he had to fight with all he had to control his urge to splash mayhem all across Texas. He had taken the whiskey from Hatfield, hoping it would calm him. Now the spirits were fueling a fire in his belly. He wanted to rip the arms off any filthy dog that even thought about touching Cassie Bohn. Thank God they were three days hard ride distant.

He read on.

Joan's letter went on and told him how this stranger who came to the rescue had dazzled Cassie.

"… *calls himself Perry Long, and claims to be Martha's long- lost cousin. Oh, he's a charmer. Dapper dresser, too. A real*

Fancy Dan. It's like he's cast a spell on Cassie. But it looks to me like what he's interested in is that trust fund Martha left for Davis. Now, this Mr. Long says he's thinking about staying on. Claims he's interested in helping his nephew, Davis. But I'm not so sure about him. He's been asking a lot of questions about Martha's will. Seems to me he's awful interested in the fact of Cassie being the trustee for Davis, with control over the funds. And with Perry Long claiming to be a relative, it wouldn't surprise me if he decided to challenge that will, saying he's a relative, so he should be made trustee.

I've tried talking sense to Cassie about it. She won't hear a word against him. Ever since that gang assaulted her, all she can see about this Perry Long is that he's her knight in shining armor. But I have a funny feeling about those men he chased off. Wouldn't surprise me if they were still in the territory.

I'm worried, Ben. About a lot of things going on here. I respect you for deciding to leave. I understand why you did it. But it would be a great comfort if you were to come out for a visit. I trust your judgment. And I hope I'm wrong. But I'm worried for Davis. For Cassie, too.

And it's about time you met Slade. Cassie's a great mother. But maybe a man like you could be a good influence.

Well, I've said enough. I know you'll do what you think is best, like you always do.

With my love,

Joan

Ben stuffed the letter back in the envelope, and stuck it in his pocket. It didn't surprise him some fella had finally come along and showed an interest in Cassie. To go by what Joan had said, she looked as good as ever. He pushed that thought out of his mind.

This particular fella, though, trying to court her? That was disturbing. But what really put a chill in Ben's spine was this 'gang' Joan had spoken about. If she was right, if they were still in the area, there'd have to be more trouble. He knew how men like that thought. The idea that some dandy ran them off wasn't something they would just forget. They might get it in their heads to come back after this Perry Long. Or Cassie, for that matter. There wasn't much of anything that could stop their kind.

Not unless Ben rode back into Texas to set things right.

Part Two

Texas

CHAPTER SIX

It was a hard ride to Pendleton. Not just because the trail was rough and dangerous. The thing that gave Ben a bigger problem was time. Time to think about Cassie. Time to remember things he had tried to push away for close to sixteen years …

Ben's best friend, Gary Bohn, had been laid to rest six days after he was shot and killed by Harvey Parson. Ben had not been there when the killing took place. He'd reached the ranch ten minutes after Gary had died, and Harvey had fled the scene with his gang. What he knew about the moments leading to Gary's death had come from Cassie, and only in bits and pieces. But there was no question in her mind about who had pulled the trigger. Harvey Parson.

Ben waited with the sobbing widow but was itching to set out to arrest Harvey as soon as Joan and her husband, Caleb, arrived at the ranch to sit with Cassie. Joan would comfort her. But Caleb, who had retired as a bounty hunter when he had married Joan, would stand guard.

As he was about to leave in pursuit of Harvey, Ben took a last look at Cassie. All he wanted was to sit down at her side. He wanted to wail and cry over Gary just as Cassie was doing. But the thought that Gary's killer, Harvey Parson, was out there on the run gave Ben the will to leave the ranch and go after the killer.

Reading the tracks in the yard, Ben could see that the surviving gang members had taken off riding to the West. But the tracks of Harvey's horse went east. Back toward town. Why?

Ben rode hard into town and went to Martha and Harvey's house. Weeping Martha, toddler Davis at her heels, told him Harvey had come and gone. He ran in, grabbed some stuff, and left in a big hurry. Ben asked her to go through what Harvey had taken. She listed what she could remember. His rifle, a second pistol, ammunition, and every red cent of cash in the house. When she had asked Harvey what was wrong, he had shoved her roughly out of the way.

"When I asked him what was wrong, he shoved me aside. I'm afraid, Ben. Why is he running?"

Ben didn't reply. He needed answers, not questions. "Any idea where he'd be headed?"

"I asked him. What he said was 'Back where I belong, woman.' I don't understand what he meant by that."

"That's all?"

"No …" Martha said, and a tear rolled out. "He stopped, just before he went out the door. He walked back over to me. Davis was crying, trying to hide behind my skirts. Harvey crouched down and picked him up very gently. And he said: 'Davis, I have one thing to leave with you. Never grow up to be like your father.' Then he kissed him on the head, handed him back to me, and was off."

"Thank you," said Ben, turning to leave.

"Ben … It's bad trouble, isn't it?"

"Worst kind. He killed a man."

Her hand flew to her mouth. "Oh no. Who?"

"Gary Bohn." He turned again, headed out the door.

Martha called after him, "Ben. If you can … bring him back. Alive. Please"

He answered without looking back, "If I can."

Ben felt lucky. Harvey's horse had a bad shoe, left rear. It made following the horse's tracks almost too easy. Plus, it might slow Harvey down a bit. Ben pushed Skip hard. He was a big horse and very strong-winded. There were plenty of horses who could outsprint Skip. For a mile. Maybe two. But then, Ben's horse just kept going, full-out. Never slowing, Skip kept galloping, kept closing, until he caught whatever he was chasing.

Harvey had a good head start.

After four miles, Ben had Harvey in sight.

Ben knew where Harvey was heading. There were some rocky badlands ahead, piles of boulders, sharp-cut stream beds. A hundred places where a bad step could kill a horse, and maybe the rider, too. He couldn't allow Harvey to reach this maze of rocks before

Ben, or he could set up an ambush. Ben pushed Skip even harder. He needed to catch Harvey before he made it into the rocks and canyons now half a mile ahead.

Ben closed to within twenty feet, when Harvey drew a gun and tried a wild shot behind him. Ben pulled his six-gun, cocked it, and yelled, "Stop, Harvey. I don't want to shoot you." Harvey answered with another wild shot, barely even looking back as he twisted around to fire.

All of a sudden, from the rocks ahead, several guns began to fire at once. The gang. They must have been holed up in the rocks, under cover. Firing away as their target got closer and closer. Ben had almost caught up to Harvey, but now the steady fire from the rocks was whizzing around him like a swarm of hornets.

"Harvey! Stop!" But Parson turned back to try one more shot.

Before Harvey could fire, Ben put a bullet in his head. Parson tumbled out of the saddle, dead before he hit the ground. Ben stopped, although Harvey's nag kept running toward the gang hidden in those rocks.

The firing kept up as Ben threw himself off Skip. Bullets kicked up sand and whanged off rocks all around him. Ben picked up Harvey's body, threw it over his horse, then jumped up and spurred Skip for home.

He let the horse slow down some now. After all, he was carrying an extra hundred and seventy pounds of dead weight. The gang kept up firing for a few more wasted shots, but Ben was out of range now. He thought about whether they would come riding after him. He knew they wouldn't. They were rustlers, bushwhackers, and back shooters. But they were also cowards, every one of them. They wouldn't come back. They'd be gone from the county before the next sunrise.

***

But the memory of that killing was only part of what tormented Ben. Killing the outlaw was part of his job. What happened after, with Cassie, was not.

It was the night after Gary's burial. Cassie held up strong through the service, as silent tears made her cheeks shine in the warm sunshine. It was nearly impossible to square a day so beautiful with a moment so dark. He stood right next to Cassie at the grave site. As the coffin was lowered into the earth, she reached out and grasped his hand.

She stayed resolute—until the first shovel of dirt hit her husband's coffin. Then she let out an ear-splitting wail of misery and began to fall in a swoon. Ben was able to catch her before she dropped to the ground. A gasp rippled the crowd. Ben swept Cassie up into his arms and carried her through the gawking mourners, grumbling at them, "Give us room. Back away, please. Give her some space." He carried her to the shade of an oak, and gently set her down in the cool grass. People began to close in, concerned, and mostly curious. "Back off!" Ben snapped, and they scurried off for a distance.

Ben's sister Joan approached with a cup of water and a cool, wet cloth. She stopped short when Ben's blazing eyes caught her own. She barely recognized the furious look on his face. It was like a savage dog, guarding his wounded master and ready to fight to the death. But then, Ben suddenly softened his stare. "Joan," he said, as if he only just that moment recognized his own sister. He beckoned her to them, and she knelt by Cassie and gently helped revive her friend.

Joan and Caleb took Cassie back to the ranch in their buggy, as Ben rode alongside silently on Skip. They got Cassie settled into the ranch house. Ben stayed at her side as Joan puttered around making tea. Caleb went outside, checking all the outbuildings, just to make sure nobody was lurking. They all stayed with Cassie until after the sun went down. Around 8:30, Joan cleaned up after the tea and biscuits. "Boys, you all get going.

Give this poor thing some peace. I'll tuck her into bed and watch over her tonight."

"I'll just stay to keep a watch," Caleb volunteered.

"Oh stop. All of you," Cassie said. She had gotten some control over the grief, for the moment. "I'll be perfectly fine. Really. Please, go on home."

"Don't be silly, dear," Joan said. "I'm not leaving you alone tonight."

"Yes, you are. Please, Joan. Alone is just what I need. Seriously. I'll be fine on my own. Better get used to it."

"But, Cassie," Joan persisted, "Tonight? Are you sure?"

"Jooooan …" Cassie drew the name out, with a tone that was just short of a warning.

"All right, all right. I know that voice. We're going." Joan moved over to Cassie and brushed her cheek with a parting kiss. "We'll check on you first thing in the morning, though."

"That'll be fine," Cassie said.

Caleb also gave her a gentle kiss on the crown of her head, saying, "You're sure you'll be okay on your own tonight?"

"I know what I'm doing. Thank you."

As Joan and Caleb turned toward the door, Ben turned his eyes to Cassie. He could see the terrible ache—he felt the same wound in his own heart. He held her gaze for several seconds. Then he gave her a single nod, and began to turn.

"Ben?" she said softly.

Joan turned to look back. She shook her head at her brother's utter lack of grace and said plainly, "Goodness gracious, Ben. Kiss the poor woman good night, for mercy's sake. It won't kill you to show some feelings, will it?"

Ben's face went crimson. He took an awkward step closer and met Cassie's red-rimmed eyes again. Then he let up just a little on the grip he was holding on his heart and reached to take her hand.

"God bless you, Cassie. We're all here for you whenever you need us." He was just about to pull away again, when she tightened her grip on his hand, and sat up, her face closer to his. He knew what she expected, and he bent down and gently put his lips on her flushed cheek.

And as he did, she whispered in his ear, so that only Ben could hear her. "Will you come by in a bit? To check on me?" Then she sat back, and he straightened up. There was sadness in her eyes still. But something more as well. And he gave her another solemn nod.

Then the three of them left Cassie to her thoughts …

***

Skip didn't mind that Ben kept pushing hard through Texas. Ben stopped for only a few hours at a time, only when exhaustion demanded sleep. But even sleep came hard. It was as if every mile Skip carried him toward Pendleton drew Ben back farther and farther into the tangled web of feelings stuffed down inside him, like ten pounds of gear in a five-pound satchel. And every bounce and bump on the trail shook that bag a little harder, and let just a little more of the past spill out.

Ben guided Skip through the bright midnight moon shining on Cassie Bohn's ranch. He tried to check the rush of conflicted emotions that raced through him, as he remembered Cassie asking him to come check on her tonight. There should be nothing wrong with that. She needed company. So did he. But what he remembered was the hot excitement of her breath, close on his neck. The feel of heat passing over his ear. As he tied Skip to a rail, he felt a nervous swell of blood rush through him. He knocked once on the door.

She was wearing a long nightshirt. A man's nightshirt. Gary's, he knew. Later, she would admit she wore it every night since he'd been shot. It still smelled like Gary.

She smiled, and they sat together. She poured herself a glass of sherry, and he joined her. It was just the one glass, he'd remember. There was no blaming what happened on the sherry.

For an hour, they talked about Gary. Laughing, crying, reveling in the joy that the grinning, open-hearted man had shared with them. With everyone. Gary was a light that shone on everybody. It was a light that somehow made everyone look just a little better. He brought out the best of people.

"You know," she said, "he really did his best for you."

"Sure he did. He was like that."

"No, I mean he was very sincere about pleading your case."

"My case?"

"Like you don't remember?" She looked at the blank innocence on his face, and reached out to run her hand over his cheek. "You were always so reserved. Still are."

He felt the heat rise in his cheek at her touch. "Gary was a good talker."

"He was. And he was right. You're a fine man. With a good heart. And a terrible job." A tear filled the corner of her eye and escaped. "Sometimes playing it safe looks like the right thing. Maybe that's a mistake."

When her lips found Ben's, he started to give in. Then drew back. "Cassie. I don't think it's right to …"

"No, nothing is right. Not now. I had right, and he's gone. I just want to get through to the morning with someone I care about." This time, when she kissed him, he reached out for her embrace. And, for a just a few hours, that's all there was.

Next morning, as Ben rode back into town, a terrible guilt grew like a cancer inside him. His best friend was barely in the ground. And he had just made love to Gary's widow. It was a terrible thing, disgraceful. People would find out. This wasn't a thing that could stay secret, not in a place like Pendleton. Because it would happen again. He was thinking about it already. And that made him feel even worse. Knowing how wrong it was, and knowing he could never keep his hands off her.

But there was no way he could ever get away with this kind of thing. He was the sheriff. People looked for him to set an example. This kind of scandal would finish him as a lawman. And it should, he thought. He was no longer fit to tell other folks how to behave.

Then he thought about what it would mean to Cassie. Once the hens in town started to cluck, it would get worse and worse. She'd be scorned. Shunned. The last thing she needed now was for folks to cut her off. It would destroy her. He couldn't allow that to happen.

Another thing bothered him. People thought he was a hero now, after he had killed the outlaw and run his gang off. They held him in high regard. And the higher a man went, the more folks seemed to relish bringing him low. Once word got out, it would not just ruin Cassie's reputation, and his own, it would also tarnish the office of sheriff itself. Turn it to something shameful and suspicious. That would make a dangerous job even worse. Not just for himself, but for anyone who took his place.

Making it worse, when he got back to town, there was a telegram waiting for him. Some fellow named Nels Erwin wanted to come down from Amarillo to interview him for the *Star*. The newspaper was planning a big story on the brave lawman who took on a whole gang. The idea filled him with dread. A reporter, poking around, talking to folks, blowing things out of proportion. And who knew what else the fellow might discover? Suppose he wanted to talk to the grieving widow. Why, of course he would. The story of a hero needed a victim, and a villain. Ben worried and stewed about it all day.

He didn't expect things could get much worse. They did. By nightfall, he would make up his mind to leave town for good. Leave Texas, leave everything behind him. It started late that afternoon.

A cattle drive had finished up herding their cows into the stockyard by the railroad. And then the drovers did what they did whenever they got a few coins in their pockets. They looked for trouble. Rot-gut whiskey, fallen doves, and all manner of dangerous idiocy. It was a given.

It took less than an hour after the trail-beaten ruffians hit the saloons, before a fistfight broke out. It was just the two of them—for now. Lots of shouting and threats, then some pushing and shoving, and the pinwheeling fists flying at each other, and most likely making very little contact.

One thing Ben had learned—break it up fast or the madness would slosh over into the other drunks. First there would be the hooting and hollering for the fight. Men would take sides. Make bets. And that urge to fight would spread. Before long there'd be a riot.

But get in between the first two, before either one took much damage, and it was easier to break them up. Easy for both men to save face. They could each boast that they would have kicked the other guy's backside, only the law interfered. Made them stop. They could turn their fury to a different wrong—the unfairness of the bully with a badge. He'd stopped them from teaching that other polecat a lesson. Truth was, both men were usually only too happy for the excuse to quit fighting. Usually.

This time it didn't go as usual.

By the time Ben made the scene, there were two dozen tipsy morons goading the pugilists on. Worse, he saw one man collecting money. Bets. Now they all had a stake in seeing the fight to a finish.

Ben wasted no time. He grabbed the nearest fighter, yanked him back, and then rammed a double stiff arm into the other guy's chest, knocking him backwards. That should have made his point, but it didn't. From behind, the first man struck Ben on the back of the head, dropping him to his knees. Then the two bruisers slammed together again, kicking, punching, gouging.

Ben staggered up, seeing stars for a moment. He shook his head, and cleared his brain. But then the anger came, hot and red, and he found his revolver in his hand. He forced reason to tamp down impulse. He fired a shot into the air, instead of dropping the two saddle tramps with .45 slugs.

"Break it up, or the next shot is going to make a hole in somebody." The two did step apart—but the big thug who had bashed him from behind now turned to launch a frontal assault. Ben easily side-stepped the wild haymaker, then gave the man a solid knock on the skull with his sidearm. The man dropped like a sack of wet sand.

Now he turned on the other fighter and leveled the barrel at his chest. "I think this fight is over now. Would you agree?"

But this was a fellow who was first in line when they were handing out stupid. The kind of stupid that gave lip to a law man pointing a gun at him. "Big man with a gun, are ya?"

"You want to go back into that saloon with your friends and have a few more sarsaparillas? Or were you planning to bunk in the jail tonight? All the same to me, mister."

One of the other trail hands spoke up now. "Listen to the man, Alabam'. He's got the drop on you."

Another cowpoke agreed. "This here's the sheriff who took down Harvey Parson."

"He don't scare me," drawled the Alabama-bred half-wit. Then he spat a wad of tobacco juice at Ben's feet. "Dare you to put that gun up, Yankee. You man enough to fight me straight up?"

"I'm man enough to know when to shut up and quit when I'm ahead."

"Quitter, are you? Figures you'd be yellow without that .45 in your hand."

Ben slowly holstered the sidearm and stared at Alabam'. "That better?"

The belligerent man smiled at Ben. "That's just fine. Now I'm gonna beat you like a rented mule."

Ben squared up and balanced on the balls of his feet. He figured the best way to fight this barrel-chested knucklehead would be quick feet, good defense, and let the chump wear himself out throwing ineffective punches.

Then Ben's mind registered something he didn't expect. The big man was going for the pistol holstered at his hip. The idiot was actually drawing down on him. But his gun wasn't halfway out of the leather when Ben drew and fired. His shot smashed the man's wrist. He fell to the ground, screaming in surprised agony.

Ben took a deep breath as the buzz of adrenaline made him feel like twitching. But he kept his voice even and measured. "Well, cowboy, which one's it going to be? Fists? Or guns?" The Alabama ox swore a curse through his gritted teeth as he continued to wail. The blood was pulsing out, and he was already weakening. Ben turned to his trail buddies. "If one of you is sober enough to help this jackass down the block," and Ben pointed, "maybe Doctor Ensel can stop the bleeding before your stupid friend gets himself a harp. Or, the alternative, I suppose."

After the crowd broke up and the Alabama ox was taken to Dr. Ensel, along with his unconscious opponent still bleeding heavily from his cracked skull, Ben went back to the sheriff's office. He passed the cells and opened the door to the simple bedroom where he'd been living for the past five years. There wasn't much in there. The bed, the desk and chair, and the chest of drawers with his clothes. The clothes were his. The furniture had all been here before Ben arrived. Before he was born, most likely. He stretched out on the bed, exhausted. But sleep was not an option. His mind was racing.

This here's the sheriff who took down Harvey Parson. That's what they'd said to the Alabama ox. For most men, that warning would make them back down.

But there were always others who wouldn't. Be they stupid, cruel, or just plain reckless, they would see Ben's new reputation as a challenge they had to meet. For a reputation of their own—whether it was to hold onto their notoriety, or earn it. And now it had started. It would only get worse.

With that thought kicking around, Ben changed focus, back to the real problem. Cassie. He ran through all the negatives again; guilt, shame, betrayal, gossip, and the certainty that no matter what he told himself, no matter what was right, no matter how it would damage Cassie—he would not, could not keep away from her. What had started between them was never going to stop as long as he was in Pendleton.

He tried to imagine the best-case scenario. They managed to lie low. They held off sleeping together for a decent time. Six months? A year? Was that possible? And even if it was, then what? They could marry. Live together as man and wife …

Until the next cattle drive, or the next train brought another gun-happy daredevil to town. It was already happening. And if that muckraker from the *Amarillo Star* showed up to make him famous … Then next year, or next month, or next week, Cassie would be a widow again.

He couldn't do that to her. He could not allow that to happen. She deserved more than that.

CHAPTER SEVEN

"You deserve more than that," Perry Long said to Cassie, as they strolled along the well-groomed trail the citizens of Pendleton maintained. It meandered along Baxter Springs Creek, winding along through shady cottonwoods, past bushes of wild huckleberries and riots of wildflowers. "Do not think me forward to say this, Cassie. But you are still an alluring woman, in the prime of your life."

"And you are a shameless flatterer, Mr. Long."

"Is it flattery if it's true?"

Cassie smiled. The man was charming. Handsome even, in a rugged sort of way.

Dressed like a respectable gentleman. There was an air of mystery about him. He was interesting … but who was he, exactly?

"Flattery is not intended to reveal truth," she said. "It says more about the flatterer."

"My flattery is sincere and comes from the heart."

"And you, Mr. Long. Where is it you come from?"

"Oh, here and there."

Purposely vague, Cassie thought. *Why?*

She asked, "And where is *here*? Or *there*?"

"For the past twelve years, I've been a railroad man."

"Really? Conductor? Or engineer?"

"I love the way you joke, Cassie. A clever woman."

"Are they so rare?"

"In my experience, clever people, men or women, are a rare commodity."

"And what cleverness did you bring to your railroad career?"

"I would say my ability to evaluate things. And people." And Long began to describe a life he had never lived, nor would he want to. "What I evaluated for various railroad enterprises was land. I would follow the initial surveyors, who found the best route to lay track. My job was to obtain rights to the land the railroad needed. Evaluate a fair price, and negotiate with ... well, anyone that wanted to sell."

"And how did you negotiate with the owners who didn't care to sell?"

"I know what you are asking. Am I an ethical man? No doubt, you have heard stories of railroad men who would stop at nothing to get what they're after."

"Not just stories."

"No. I fear you are right. There were times I was not successful buying a desirable parcel. But my way around these dilemmas was to seek an alternative solution. By which I mean, find land with a willing seller."

"And if no such alternative was available?"

Perry Long took a moment. "I am intrigued by your persistence in testing my motives, Cassie. Where does such curiosity come from?"

"From experience, sir. Too much experience." They walked in silence a moment. Then she asked, "So, I take it you have left the railroad."

"Correct. And the truth is, in fact, I left disillusioned. In part for the very questionable business practices you disapprove. For I feel the same. And there came a point when conscience called me to change directions."

"I see. So it is conscience, then, which called you to Pendleton?"

"In a way, yes, you could say that. Ours was a small family, and to be frank, not all that close knit. I thought I was the first one to try my mettle in the West. I didn't know my cousin Martha had set out for the new frontier. I only learned it by chance when I was in Fort Worth." Here, Perry inserted a most realistic sigh. "My great regret is that my journey here to reunite with her was too late. It seems a cruel fate." He then took a brighter tone. "But not without a silver lining, if you will. Nothing could make me happier than to discover my nephew, Davis. I feel it my duty to help look out for him. What a fine young man. What a credit to his parents."

"To his mother, at any rate."

"You took a dim view of his father?"

"He killed my husband."

"Good God! Are you serious?"

Cassie didn't answer. Then, finally, she said "It was a long time ago."

"But … how very strange. I mean, Davis, you're so close to him. And he says you were a good friend to Martha. How is it possible?"

"Sins of the father are not sins of the son. Or the wife, I guess."

Perry Long stopped. He looked into her eyes and delicately took her hands as he said, "Cassie, you are really the most remarkable woman. And that is not mere flattery. I am deeply moved by your fine character."

"I believe that no person is all good or all bad. Some are better at choosing the right path. And some are drawn in the wrong direction."

***

At that moment, twenty-two miles to the southwest, Ben found himself at a fork in the road. There were no signposts. And he did not clearly remember which way would take him to Pendleton. He stopped and tried to recall something, anything, a feature or landmark that might help.

He shook his head, and patted his horse on the neck. "Well, Skip, what do you think? Flip a coin?" Skip snorted, blowing Texas dust out of his nose. "Wish Old Hank was here. He'd know the way."

And at this, Skip picked up, trotting directly down the center of the trail on the right, as if there was a whole boxcar full of oats at the end the road. Ben smiled. "Your guess is as good as mine, I reckon."

Caleb was out in front of the ranch house, filling a bucket of water for Joan, who aimed to do some laundry. The squeak of the pump handle reminded him again that he needed to oil it. He gave the noisy lever a final push, and the bucket was full. When the sound of the water ended, that's when he heard the clop of hooves approaching. He turned as he stood. He squinted into the sun, which was low behind the rider. As he got a look at the man's face, he was uncertain for a moment. Could it be?

"Your ears are getting old, Caleb," Ben teased. "If I was a Comanche, you'd be one sorry ex-bounty hunter."

"JOAN!" Caleb shouted toward the ranch house.

Skip walked straight up to the bucket and started slurping down the water.

"Thanks for having a drink ready for my horse," Ben said as he swung down from the saddle. He did a shivery little shake to get some blood back in his backside.

Caleb threw his arms around Ben. Clouds of dust filled the air as he pounded Ben's back like he was beating a carpet. "JOAN!" he hollered again. Then he looked at Ben's horse, and rubbed his eyes. "God Almighty, Ben. That can't be Old Hank."

"This here? He's Skip."

"Spitting image, though."

"I know what I like in a horse, is all."

"JOAN!" he called again and this time she came out of the ranch house, her feet moving at quick march, and her tongue doing the same.

"Caleb Norris, I'm in there ready to wash your smelly old shorts, and you're out here jawboning with some sorry-looking saddle tramp while his swayback mule is drinking up my laundry water! I'd like to know just what's got into …"

And then Joan saw it was Ben standing there. She let out an ear-splitting shriek of joy. "Aaaaah! Ben! Is it really you!?!"

Ben nodded once. "Howdy, Joan."

Even if he had been planning to say more, he missed the opportunity. His sister was hugging him, kissing him, laughing, weeping, and dragging him into her kitchen "to put some meat on your bones."

After his long stint on the trail, Ben was only too happy to let his sister stuff him full of fried chicken, soda bread, beans, tortilla, corn, beets, some bacon and eggs, a slice of pecan pie, and another slice of cherry pie. Then she offered to bake an apple pie, too.

"Well," Ben said, pushing back from the table. "Sure. We can save it for tomorrow."

And while he wolfed down the sensible snack, she also fed him her worries about Cassie and "that slick-talking peacock Perry Long. Last few days, he's keeping company and then some," she told him. "To me, it looks like he's courting her. Spends almost all his time mooning around the ranch. He claims that's so he can be near his nephew. But I don't buy a word of it."

"You saying he's living out there?" Ben said, darkening.

"No, not that. Wouldn't put anything past him, though. But he's staying in town. Fact is, he set himself up in Martha's house like he owns the place. I'm sure he's been snooping around every inch, trying to find hidden jewels or a chest of gold doubloons."

"Is that what he's after, do you think. The house?"

"I'm with Joan on this one," Caleb spoke up. "I'd say there's nothing of value Perry Long ain't after getting. Reminds me of a carpetbagger."

"Maybe I'll just take a closer look at the fella myself."

"Ask me, you'd be doing Cassie a favor." Joan looked Ben in the eye and added, "You'd be doing right by that son of hers."

Ben broke his gaze with Joan, and turned to Caleb. "What about these saddle bums? Have you seen 'em?"

"The ones who went after Cassie? No, I never did. Wasn't in town when it happened. Far as I know, they ain't been back since."

"Maybe. I'll scout around."

"I can ride with you."

"No you don't," Ben said. He smiled at Joan. "I don't aim to open that nest of fire ants."

"It's this Perry Long that worries me," Joan said again.

"I'll look into that, too."

Joan smiled, then almost began to cry. She threw her arms around her brother. "Oh, Ben. I'm just so happy you're here. I've missed you so. And this town's missed you. We have a drunkard for a sheriff here nowadays."

"Oh no. I ain't ever putting on a badge again."

"We know that, Ben," Caleb said, with a sharp look at his wife. "Joan's just saying Pendleton could use a sober sheriff. This Ingram Oldham is pickled from sunrise to midnight."

"So I figure he didn't bother to follow up on those men?"

"Not unless they stole a barrel of whiskey. And even if they had, he might just have joined up with the gang until it was all gone."

"Guess I'll drop by the jailhouse anyway. Courtesy."

"Waste of time, but you'll do whatever," said Caleb. "I bet that's one thing ain't changed, and ain't going to."

"First thing, though, I'll take a ride by Cassie's."

"Do that, Ben. Maybe you can put some sense in her head about this weasel sniffing around."

"We'll see," Ben said, and he went out to saddle up Skip.

CHAPTER EIGHT

Cassie had an apron on to make sure she didn't mess up her best dress. She bustled around the small parlor, which was already as neat and clean as it could be. She rearranged throw pillows on the couch, stepped back for a look, then put them back the way they had been.

She went to the kitchen windowsill, to check the cherry pie cooling there. The crust was brown and flaky. She was known in particular for her light, melt-in-your-mouth pie crust. She was glad she had sent Slade and Davis off to go fishing. They would have been hanging around like starved dogs, sniffing around that pie, whining for just one slice to split between them. And even when she shooed them off, she'd probably find a little pinch had been snitched off the edge of the crust. Best they were off the ranch altogether for now.

She sat down at the table, took a small fan from her sleeve, and tried to fan some cool on her face. It didn't help. Not that she gave it much of a chance. Two minutes after she sat, she was up, bustling into the kitchen to rearrange the tea tray, make sure the silver sugar bowl was full, sniffing to be certain the cream was still good and fresh.

She also had a coffee pot handy, if that turned out to be something Perry Long preferred over tea. But it was her impression that someone who dressed like such a gentleman was someone who customarily took tea in the afternoon. But either way, she was ready to see that he was well taken care of.

She moved into her bedroom and up to her mirror. First, she stood back far enough that she could make a thorough review of herself head to feet. She frowned at the dowdy look the apron gave her and whisked it off. Now she could see her dress, all crisp and clean. And she could give her figure a critical once-over. Not bad at all, she thought. She moved in closer, giving her face a close examination. There were worry lines, she couldn't deny that. Not deep; barely so you'd notice. Nothing a little touch of powder wouldn't mitigate.

She was just about to apply another little touch—she'd already done a full face and hair primp, but it didn't hurt to freshen up, she thought, when she heard footsteps on the wood porch at the front of the house.

She darted a quick peek at the clock over on her dresser. A beautiful mechanism, ticking away under a tall glass cylinder with a rounded dome top. It had been the finest wedding gift she and Gary had gotten. You could see all the wheels and springs and gears inside, the movement a marvelous animation. And she knew it was fully wound, so the time it displayed should be accurate. Which meant her expected caller, Perry Long, was quite early. She heard a soft tap-tap on the front door and gave her cheeks a fast pinch. She left the mirror and glided breezily toward the door, not at all unhappy that Perry was ahead of schedule. She pulled open the door with a beaming smile on her face.

The instant she saw Ben standing there, Cassie's tongue seized up. She opened her mouth, then quickly closed it again. It was so dry her tongue seemed to be glued to the roof of her mouth.

Ben nodded once. "Cassie," he said softly, as he swept the hat from his head, and smiled. After a moment of awkward stillness, he looked past her, surveying the familiar parlor, neat as a pin. "You look real nice," he managed. Then he noticed the dark bruise under her eye and on her cheek. The face powder did a lot to disguise it, but there was the evidence. A surge of fury flashed up like a prairie fire, and he held back a curse.

"L— Lu—" she stammered, then tried to get enough spit to swallow. "Ben," she finally croaked. "I … When did you—"

"Rode in this morning." Then he couldn't hold back. "Damn them. Look at your face." He reached gently for her cheek but stopped before taking the liberty of touching her. She saw his hand was literally trembling with rage.

"Oh, don't make a fuss. It's well on the mend."

"I'll find the men who have done this outrage."

"Ben. Please. They're gone. It's over and done with."

"If that's what they think, they'll learn different."

"That is not required, sir. But thank you."

"It's the only way that will satisfy me, knowing you're safe from them."

"I'm safe enough. They won't be back."

"I'll make certain of it."

"Please. Don't worry. I'm well protected. Davis Madden is near as tall as you, I'd reckon. He's staying with us, with Martha being gone."

"Joan has told me."

"And Slade—you'll have to see him. Almost fully grown. And perhaps near the equal of Caleb at target shooting."

"Shooting at men who are shooting back is a very different thing. As Caleb will tell you any day of the week."

"I'm not expecting any gunplay."

"But I do not see your young protectors standing watch."

"They're off. Fishing. They'll be back before dark."

Ben looked around at the pristine furniture, the wood floor polished to a gleam. He noted the pie in the window, the tea tray ready for deployment. He saw how she had primped herself up for … *For what?* he wondered. *For whom?*

"You look like …" he stammered at last.

"Don't say 'like the last time you saw me'. Please."

"Well, yes. You do. But I was meaning to say you look like company is expected.

And I'm very sure it ain't me." He stepped back and began to put his hat back on his head. "I'm sorry. I'm interrupting. Perhaps I can call again."

She reached out suddenly, grasping his wrist. "Ben, wait …"

"Is your visitor this man Joan spoke of to me? The one who chased off the ruffians, to save the day?"

She felt a funny sort of guilt—there was no reason for it, she told herself. "His name is Perry Long, and he was poor Martha's cousin."

"So I understand."

"And I think it's been a good thing for Davis, his uncle turning up. So he doesn't feel he has no family at all."

"Quite a lucky chance this Long showed up out of nowhere, then."

"What are you suggesting?" Ben could hear a huffy tone rising.

"I'm suggesting that today does not appear to be a convenient time to show up here, out of the blue." He nodded once. "Would I be welcome at a better time?"

"Welcome? Ben, of course. I'm so happy you're in town. I can't wait to catch up with you. Oh, and you must meet the boys. Perhaps tomorrow?"

"I'll be back, then." That one nod again, and he headed for his horse. She watched him trot off back toward town. A strange feeling fluttered inside her, one that had been lost for so very long. Then she went back inside and moved the pillows on the couch again.

***

Ben was halfway to town when he saw the man sitting in a fine-looking buggy, moving toward him. Even from fifty yards, it was clear the fellow was a dandy. He was all got up, fine as you please. Just as Cassie had been.

So. This is him.

As they grew closer to one another, each man plastered a smile on his face. Both of which signaled a bonhomie that was worse than false. The smiles were intentionally deceitful. Perry Long didn't know Ben Moss at all, and had no reason not to display friendly intentions. But inside, Arno Parson knew exactly who he was just about to pass.

The man who had killed his brother, Harvey. A man who Arno was anxious to send to his own bloody end.

And as they passed close by each other, Ben didn't know why he felt a hot, glowing hatred burning inside him. It must be jealousy, he told himself. And true, the thought of this dandified interloper laying claim to Cassie did infuriate him. Though he had no right to the feeling. He had taken off without a word to her, almost sixteen long years ago. He had forfeited any right or claim.

But for some reason, as he gave a passing glance directly at the man's clean-shaven face, something else sent a flush of cold bile into his belly. The kind of feeling that he got in the fraction of a second before he saw a man go for his gun. The feeling that gave Ben the only edge he would get to shoot first. He slowed Skip. Came to a stop and tried to concentrate—what was sending this subconscious alarm through his every nerve? He turned his horse halfway around and looked at the back of the retreating figure. This Perry Long, trotting his fancy buggy down the lane, to call upon a handsome widow, Mrs. Cassie Bohn. Ben had an almost overwhelming urge to ride him down and beat the truth out of him. For, whatever that truth was, Ben was certain this man kept it buried inside, behind that false smile and fancy outfit.

Then Ben let the feeling pass and turned Skip back toward town.

At the same time, in his buggy, as Arno passed Ben Moss, his hand drifted down to the fine, shiny pistol set in his beautiful, polished leather holster. *Pull it,* his mind screamed. *Forget the woman. Leave the money. Just do what you really need to do, and do it now. Shoot that rat in the back. Kill Ben Moss. Now.*

But each man kept going in their opposite directions. The time would come. Each of them knew it. But this was not the time.

CHAPTER NINE

Ben tied Skip to the hitching post outside the sheriff's office and went inside. The plan was to see if Sheriff Oldham had even a scrap of useful information to help Ben track down the men who had accosted Cassie. But when he stepped into the office, he noticed two things. First, the place reeked of piss and whiskey-laced vomit. Second, Ingram Oldham was nowhere to be seen.

Ben's instinct was to go look for the sheriff in a saloon. There were seven of them in Pendleton, so it took almost an hour to hit the right gin mill. Oldham, it turned out, was a creature of habit. He began the morning at Gil's Ale House, where he could get a beer with a raw egg cracked in it. Breakfast. He'd been there, and gone.

Next, he went to either Bob's Beef and Bar, or to Steed's Saloon and Grill, where he'd wash down a hunk of tough steak with almost enough whiskey to kill the taste. 'Almost' only because even an infinite amount of rot gut was not quite capable of completely erasing the gamey flavor of Steed's tainted beef, or Bob's, either, for that matter. But Oldham had already moved on.

Steed advised Ben that the sheriff always ended his day at The Grand Pendleton, as it offered rooms for lodging, although these were dedicated to accommodating the traffic and commerce of Janet "Lady Jane" Varney. And the women of negotiable morals Jane represented. The sheriff liked the idea of having that option at the end of his long day of intoxication. But, Ben figured, it was too early for that particular dive.

This left three he had not checked, and that was when he got lucky. He did 'Eeny-meeny-miney-mo', and went to Whit's Whiskey Bar. Bingo.

And that was where his luck also ended. Oldham was conscious, at least. Even sociable and cooperative. But ultimately as useless as horseshoes on a buzzard.

"Them scoundrels?" he mumbled. "Why, they lit out of town quicker than a dog will eat a cat turd. I expect they heard what kind of holy hell I'd have brought down, and skedaddled pronto. My professional conclusion would be they're either holed up someplace out in them badlands, or more likely, well past the county line and good riddance."

"Thanks for all your help," Ben said, trying to maintain a minimal respect for the office of sheriff, if not for the inebriated office holder.

"Say, Ben is it? Fella with your name used to wear a star around here. That wouldn't be you, would it? I'd be proud to stand a fellow officer of the law to a little nip of the nectar."

"I'm not your man." And Ben left, to make the rounds of the shopkeepers on the street where the ruffians had committed their molestation. He got a fair description of a little man with a knife, then a big fat man who sounded like a foreigner; German maybe? There was a redheaded man, and one fellow who stood a head taller than the rest, with a head of long, matted black hair that went halfway down his enormous back, and a bird's nest of a beard, also black, with a little bit of gray coming in around the mouth. That one sounded like the fellow on a wanted poster he'd seen every time he'd gone into the Express Office back home in Truth or Consequences. Jerry Quincy. And from what Ben had heard, Quincy was running with a gang of men under Arno Parson.

He still didn't know where to find them. But now he knew who he was looking for. And he planned to hunt them, find them, and put them down like rabid coyotes.

***

After their chance encounter on the road to town, Perry Long paid a visit to Cassie out at her ranch. He had news. The telegram he had sent to Amarillo had been answered. Foster Bass, the circuit judge, was on his way to Pendleton already, and had calendared a reading of Martha Madden's last will and testament in two days, on Wednesday morning, at the land office.

"Good," said Cassie. "From Martha, I pretty much know what's in it."

"Really? That's interesting."

"I shouldn't talk about it, though."

"And I admire your fidelity to Martha's final wishes. I'm sure she's provided well for my nephew, Davis. He's a bright young man, lots of promise."

"Well, as you are his uncle, it doesn't hurt, I suppose, to tell you that you're right about that. Martha put everything into a trust. It will provide for all Davis' living expenses and a small allowance to cover his expenses for the period until his majority."

"Twenty-one, that would be? He's what now, seventeen, I believe?"

"Seventeen going on thirty."

"I know what you mean. Davis is quite a mature young man. Sensible."

"And the trust will provide for his education expenses. He plans to study the law."

"That's excellent. I am so happy he's not only provided for but has such a sensible plan for his future."

"He's a great kid. And a wonderful friend to my boy, Slade. I'm thrilled he's living with us, at least until he leaves for his studies. We'll miss him."

"I'm sorry I was too late to reunite with poor Martha. But I give thanks that she had a loyal friend like you, Cassie."

"We have always loved Davis like our own."

"That means so much to me," Perry Long said with all the conviction he could put into his lies. "Again, I say, you are the most remarkable woman, Cassie."

"And you, sir, are still an incorrigible flatterer."

At this, he reached for her hand and gazed into her eyes. "Cassie, I know we haven't been acquainted long, but I know you're a wonderful mother. And a strong, capable woman. Not to mention an attractive one."

Cassie withdrew her hand from his and got up off the sofa. Hiding the smile she wanted to release, a most girlish feeling she admitted to herself, she bustled into the kitchen to change the atmosphere and keep her cool. "Perry Long, if you don't stop trying to turn my head, I swear I'll …"

When she didn't finish, Perry prompted her. "What? What will you do if I continue to speak truth, directly from my heart?"

"Ignore your foolishness and make us a cup of tea, is what."

But that didn't stop the feeling she was trying to put under wraps. It had been a long time … much too long … since she'd had a gentleman press his luck with her. It felt wonderful.

And then, an unbidden thought flashed through her mind: *It's too bad Ben doesn't have such feelings.*

***

Arno spent the next hour at her side, spinning all manner of fantasy about the hopes and plans of Perry Long for the future. Perry said Martha's untimely demise, and the realization that he had family here in Pendleton, had made him realize time was passing. That his nomadic life had led him on a long chase after he knew not what. But now, he did know—he had learned to listen to the voice inside, which was telling him the time had come to settle down. And having Davis here had made him feel that Pendleton might be the right place to do it. "I see myself here, taking a wife, having a family."

"Well, I think that's a very normal impulse for a man who has matured. As you have, clearly."

"I have indeed. And I don't wish to be too forward, Cassie. So I will only say how happy it would make me to find that life. A man who has been too long a rolling stone needs to catch up. Perhaps I should look for a family well on its way already, with nothing missing but a loving husband and father." Then he stood, wishing he could make himself blush, and turned away because even he couldn't lie that well. "But, forgive me. I've gone too far, and said too much, too soon. Please don't let me prattle on with such indiscretion. I will only embarrass both of us."

"Oh, don't be so harsh with yourself, Perry. I understand well enough how one can climb up on a fantasy horse, only to find it galloping off out of control."

"I will try to rein in my feelings, then, Cassie. For now …"

With that, he began to reach for her hand again. But Cassie got to her feet and walked to the window, taking in the breathtaking sunset, filled with bright reds and golds, purples, maroons, whitish silvery strands—so many glowing colors beyond naming. "Those boys ought to be back any second now. I told them sunset, and they know I mean business." And she kept vigil in the window, not letting herself return her attention to the flattering suitor trying to court her.

She didn't wait even a minute when she spotted the boys on their way home. They were spurring their mounts to a near-gallop, determined to make it home before the dying rays of the afternoon disappeared completely.

And shortly after their return, with a line of fine, fat fish from the river, Perry Long pleaded his regrets and declined the invitation to dinner that Davis blurted out, without even asking how Cassie might feel about another mouth to feed. She never did mind, after all. But Perry Long had to take his leave.

Because Arno Parson had other business concerning him.

***

Ferd Martinez had not lived thirty-seven years on the outside of a jail—and without a rope around his neck—by taking chances. So he had ordered the five other gang members to remain hidden among the rocky gullies and canyons of the badlands. He rode out alone to meet Arno Parson in a moonlit clearing a mile outside town.

Arno had new information and new instructions to share with his second in command. He knew he could count on Martinez. He was the one member of the gang with sense enough to pour piss out of a boot. He was crafty, and risk averse. And his loyalty was unquestioned.

Parson told him the best news first. He had found Ben Moss. And Moss didn't even know who Parson was. When the time was right, Arno would be able to pounce without warning and get his hands on Ben. Then he planned to draw out his revenge until the last agonizing second of life dripped out of the man who had killed Harvey.

The icing on the cake was his plan to get control of the Madden kid's trust fund. He had two alternatives, and either one might work. First, he chuckled. The widow, who was likely to be named executor and trustee, was already getting sweet on him. If the trust fell under her control, he would do all that was necessary to gain control over her. Threats to her own son if need be, but with a proposal of marriage as the preferred subterfuge. And he would be a very willing husband when it came time to consummate the marriage, before draining the trust and vanishing with the proceeds.

But first he would try to take the most direct route. It was a delicate matter, but he would try to convince the judge that, as the boy's only known living relative, giving 'Uncle Perry' control, or partial control, at least, of the trust would be in the boy's best interest. He would argue that Martha Madden would have agreed, had she known her own 'Cousin Perry' was willing to assume the duty of caring for her orphaned son. And the boy was primed to go along with Perry Long on this, he was sure. But one way or another, he wanted to get his hands on that tidy fortune.

So Arno Parson laid out his battle plans. Ben Moss was living at the ranch of his sister, Joan Norris. Martinez was to station the men nearby, where they could watch Ben's movements. If he left the ranch, Martinez should leave a rear guard to keep the ranch under surveillance, and follow Moss wherever he went. Just keep track of him. Don't kill him, don't grab him, don't do anything but keep him in their sights. Arno wanted to control the timing. Get the trust under his control first. Then drag Ben Moss to the judgment he deserved.

CHAPTER TEN

An hour after sunrise, Martinez peered carefully out of the rocky hillside vantage he had found. It was as good as a duck blind for keeping their prey under observation. And sure enough, when Ben came out from the Norris ranch house to saddle up his horse, Martinez knew it would be a simple matter to follow Ben and keep tabs on him wherever he went. And the prey would never even know he was being stalked. It was perfect.

"Stay here," he told Gandy. "If he starts to leave before I roll those lazy back shooters out of their warm blankets, signal me. Like this—" and Martinez whistled a very creditable bird call. *Whip-Poor-Will. Whip-*

Poor-Will. He made Gandy try it. It was crap, but good enough to warn Martinez if need be.

Martinez moved five yards deeper into the woods to where the gang had made cold camp. No fires, no smoke. He kicked Sammy Yost harder than necessary to wake him, and enjoyed the yowl of angry pain, which was enough noise to stir the other layabouts.

"Beauty sleep's over. On your feet and saddle your mounts," he barked at the grumbling desperados. "Not you, Ebersky. Stay here with Gandy and keep watch over the ranch, just in case."

It was easy enough for Martinez and his squad of deplorables to keep their distance when following Ben. It was obvious from early on where he was headed. To Cassie

Bohn's ranch. They trailed him there and took up watch, keeping well hidden.

***

Ben dismounted, and Davis jumped to volunteer to take Skip to the barn and get his saddle off. "Thank you, son," Ben said, moving toward the porch. He passed Slade, who was filling a bucket at the hand pump. "Your mother decent, boy?"

"Yes, sir," Slade said. "Go on, I'll be right behind you with the water. She's just fixing to make some more coffee."

Ben walked up onto the wooden porch. Before knocking at the front door, he went to the kitchen window and took a peek inside. He saw Cassie just leaving the room, with her back turned, going into her bedroom. He tried to wave, but she didn't see him.

"It's all right, sir," said Slade, now right behind him with the water bucket. "Come on inside with me, if you're of a mind to."

It was then Ben noticed the reflection of the boy in the glass of the window. Slade was slightly behind him, with the image of the boy's face side by side with his own. What he saw was so startling, he almost jumped. He checked his shock, and spent a second examining Slade's reflection, comparing it to his own. It was practically a spitting image of Ben. How had he failed to see what was so obvious? How could anyone miss it? Maybe, he thought, because I don't know my own face that well. For Ben was not a man who spent a wasted second gazing at his own reflection, even when he shaved. He watched the razor and where it was scraping off stubble, just to make sure he didn't cut himself. But he never bothered to stand back and pay even a moment's attention to the overall image of his face.

But now he did. And it was the same face as Slade Bohn.

Ben marveled. Slade looked nothing like his father. How on earth had others never noticed this? Then it occurred to Ben that Gary had been nine months under the earth before Slade was even born. And by the time Slade grew enough for anyone to notice, nobody had seen Gary's face for years. They had nothing to compare to Slade. Besides, Cassie had always told everyone what a blessing it was that she and Gary had been trying real hard to create a baby. She'd thanked God, saying that her only blessing was that Gary had planted fertile seed, perhaps even the night before he was killed. They had certainly spent plenty of time trying, every day. It was too much information for proper folks, and nobody ever even considered pressing for details. It was clearly assumed by everyone that Slade was Gary's issue.

But to Ben, that was no longer clear at all.

He followed Slade inside. The boy set the water near the stove and called to his mother that it was ready for making coffee. He also announced Ben, who was to him nearly a total stranger. And why would Slade think otherwise? He had literally never even seen the face of the dead man assumed to be his father.

"Ben. This is a surprise," she said without much welcome in her voice.

"Sorry if I'm intruding. We never set a time, but I can come back …"

"No, no. Don't be silly. Besides, I wanted you to meet the boys, and at least you're here before they get some notion to wander off and disappear until they get hungry."

"Sure. Boys." As if Ben knew anything about raising children.

"Well," she turned to Slade. "Did you and Davis introduce yourselves?" And of course, she assumed, that was far too much etiquette to expect. The proof was the way Slade dropped his eyes to the floor.

"No'm," the boy muttered, addressing his boots.

"Well, fetch Davis in here, and show Mr. Moss you were brought up here in the house. And not in that barn out there. Go!"

Slade galloped off to fetch Davis, glad to get out of the burning spotlight. Cassie shook her head and smiled at Ben. "I swear, I could do better teaching manners to a litter of wolverines."

Ben chuckled and had to admit, "No problem. Don't reckon I've ever got tamed quite as good as your average wolverine myself."

"On that point, I will not argue with you." But she smiled saying it. "I've always had a weakness for wolverines."

"'Spose you could say I didn't act much different when I left here. That was a mistake I'll regret to the day I die. I mean that, Cassie."

She tried to move past this line of conversation. "I'm just putting up some coffee. You must stay for some, of course." She made a frown. "What's keeping those boys?"

"Usual, I expect. One of them spotted a snake. Or found Comanche footprints, more likely."

"Pirates," said Cassie, correcting that notion. "Last year was Comanches. It's pirates now, generally. But if they don't get in here, somebody is going to walk the plank."

"They'll be here, by and by. Curiosity about this old friend of yours, showing up out of the blue." Meaning himself.

"They're not the only ones curious."

"I came on account of Joan asked me."

"She's your sister. Of course she'd miss you."

"Been after me for years."

"Wore you down, did she?"

"No." He stopped.

"No? That's mysterious."

"She told me she was worried about you. And Davis."

"I told you. I expect no further trouble from those saddle tramps. They were just passing through. And now they're gone in the wind."

"But not your knight in shining armor. He must see something he likes in these parts. Is that right?"

"Ben," she began, but stopped herself.

"I'm sorry. I have no right to ask anything. Not after the way I left."

"I've gotten over that. I've had to."

"I never have done so. Nearly sixteen years. I owed you an apology. And an explanation. But I can see you've done well. It does ease my mind some."

"It hasn't been easy. But Slade has made life worth living."

"He's a fine boy."

"Oh, you don't even know him. If they'd just get back, you could find out what he's like."

"I know he looks well."

"His father was a handsome man."

"Gary was a fine-looking fellow, all right."

Those words hung in the air for just a moment—then the sound of a cattle stampede—oh no, wait, those were just two sets of boots—stomped loudly up onto the porch, and the two boys burst into the house.

"Hold your horses right there!" They froze, just inside the door. "No," Cassie grumbled, "I didn't think so."

Bang, bang, clamor, clamor—a trample of boots clattered back out, followed by the sounds of boots scraping and stamping off the dust.

"All right. Come in and introduce yourselves, you hooligans."

Their faces were alive with curiosity, excitement, and exuberance. They both talked at the same time, their names mixed in a jumble and cloud of "nice to meet you" and "it's a pleasure." Then both stopped at the same time, frozen like two men trying to go through the same door at the same time.

"Hello, boys," said Ben, offering his hand in a solemn show of respect. He treated them like the men they almost were. "I'm Ben Moss."

"You were the sheriff!" Slade barked out, excited.

"You were the best sheriff ever," Davis said, to top Slade.

"I wouldn't say …"

But Slade cut him off, blurting "You were the fastest gun in Texas!"

"That's not really …"

"Sure it is," Slade interrupted. "You shot down outlaws."

"Slade!" Cassie snapped, darting a glance at Davis.

But Davis was clearly not upset. "It's all right. I know my father was an outlaw. He was a rustler and a killer, and you did right, sir."

"You killed the man who murdered my father!" Slade added. "I'm proud to meet you, sir."

Cassie felt a strange shame about what the boys were saying. They were right on the facts, but she was very uncomfortable.

Ben started to straighten them out. "Boys, I see you think it's a glamorous thing to take up the duty of sheriff. But there's a lot of complication to it. People see you wearing the badge; they all have their own feelings about that. Some folks are glad to see you. They respect you. But they expect a lot. They want you to be perfect. And no man is perfect. Least of all me."

He looked at how they took that in. Then he went on. "Other folks will resent you. Sure, they're happy to have you lay down the law—when it suits them. But only as long as you don't bother them, or their friends. But if you have to act against something, and they don't like it, why then you're a tyrant, a monster, a maniac. Out of control. Out to get them for no good reason. Understand?"

Both of them nodded. "And then you have the folks who see you as the enemy. They may be complete outlaws. Or they might only be the kind of person who says the rules are for everyone else. But not them. And for some folks, just who you are, just that badge alone—that's enough to make you a target. And you know the worst part?"

Two faces with wide-open eyes and ears shook their heads, eager to hear.

"Most of the time, you don't really know who is which kind. Because people will hide who they really are inside. And because everyone—every man, woman, and child—has all of those things inside them. Good. Evil. Love. Hate. Compassion. Cruelty. Generosity. Greed. All of us. You. Me. Your family. All of us are flawed. Some folks are better, some are worse. But every one of us has some good inside. And any one of us can give into the bad side, under the wrong circumstances. You hear what I'm telling you?"

They both blurted at the same time, "Sir." "Yes, sir."

"And, as far as killing someone who's broken the law? It's a hard and terrible thing to take on your shoulders. Because dead is dead. Kill the bad, and you also kill the good.

And then? The good and the evil are both gone. They're nothing. Nothing at all."

"Yes, sir." "Sir." Both of them were doing their best to keep a somber look on their faces.

"So here's what I'd like you to do." He looked each of them in the eye in turn. "When you see an angel, with wings and a harp, and all of that, remember that even an angel can fall. In fact, it happened to the best angel in God's heaven. And his name was Lucifer."

He saw them let those words sink in. "So all of life is part of that struggle. You can try to do good. You can struggle against evil. But you keep this in your heart. Both of those, good and evil, are inside you, too. Inside every one of us."

Ben was finished. He'd just said more words than he would normally say in a month. And he felt all talked out.

Then, from outside on the porch, they heard a slow, repeated beat. Clap … Clap … Clap … The applause was from none other than Perry Long.

He had been out there, listening. For … well, who knew how long. Long enough to spur him to delivering his sarcastic applause. "You boys can learn a lot from this fella," said Perry, stepping inside. "He's lived all of it. Good. And evil. Like every one of us imperfect souls." He beamed a realistic smile at Cassie, removed his dapper derby hat, and offered her a slight bow.

"Perry," Cassie said. "You must feel like you walked into Sunday School."

"Well, the honest truth is, maybe I should do that more often," he said. Then he turned to Ben. "It's good for every one of us to have his soul in working order. We never know when we'll be called home to the Lord. Do we?"

"Not generally," Ben responded. And the two stood staring each other down, like a pair of bucks with their antlers locked in a tangle.

Cassie couldn't bear the tension gripping the room. "I have fresh coffee on. Let's go out on the veranda and enjoy this lovely day, shall we?" The boys nearly bowled over the adults, released like arrows fully drawn. Ben and Perry each gestured for the other to go ahead, dueling with insincere politeness. Then they both moved at once and bumped one another on their way out the door to the porch.

***

Over in their hidden blind, Martinez and his fellows watched Moss and Parson step outside together. Jerry Quincy, whose mood had been darkening ever since Arno had ordered them to cold camp, was in a black mood. He wasn't fond of cold beans. Sleeping cold was something he'd hated all his life. He was grumpy without hot coffee. And worse—although no living man knew this—he had suffered in fear all night, when there was no firelight to hold off the blackness. That stimulated him to a rare expression of what he was thinking. "Shoot him, already. What the hell is he waiting for?"

"Shut up, Quincy," Martinez said quietly. "You know why."

"Sure. He wants to screw that woman," opined Sammy Yost, who was the best equipped to understand the lure of illicit lust, and how it could blind a man to anything, even his own good.

"Screw her out of that money, I'd wager", said Red. "And leaving every one of us in danger while he plays his damn games."

Martinez shook his head. No one knew it, but he'd decided this was the last caper he was going to engage in with those morons. They were all as stupid as Arno Parson was crazy. He would rather extend his record run of thirty-seven years unhanged.

CHAPTER ELEVEN

One thing the Parson gang couldn't see from up in the hidden perch was the war going on inside Arno Parson. He forced himself to sit out there on the porch with Cassie and Ben Moss. The devil on his shoulder screamed into his ear. *Kill him. Shoot him down now.*

But he knew that was foolish. It would destroy all his other plans. It would cost him the money to keep his gang happy and willing. It would dash his consuming fantasy to have his way with this woman, on his terms. It would mean that his nemesis was dead without the prolonged, suffering agony Arno dreamed of, and that would cut short the revenge that he had craved for almost sixteen years.

But the biggest negative was the danger. He could probably work a way to get a gun into his hand and blast the life out of Moss before Ben could draw his pistol and shoot Arno. It wouldn't be easy. He could tell Moss was as wary as Arno himself at this moment. And he knew Ben was fast as a hooker's wink.

But even if Arno was quick and sneaky enough to plug Moss, there were the others. Obviously, he couldn't leave witnesses. But he knew it was possible—even likely—that Cassie was once again packing that six-gun somewhere in those skirts. And she would use it. He had no doubt of that.

But even if he managed to get both of them down, then there were those two boys. Chances were he could take them, even if they armed themselves when they heard gunfire. They might already be armed, for that matter. But that was an unknown. It assumed he not only managed to kill Ben, and then Cassie, but did so without so much as a flesh wound. But if one of them got off a shot, winged him in the arm or a leg, or worse, then he would likely end up dead. A wounded man with just a pistol didn't stand a chance against two teens armed with rifles. Even if his gang sprang from hiding and raced to aid him in battle, he could be dead before the help arrived.

By the time Cassie served the coffee, Arno saw that Ben was studying his face mighty closely. Would he ever make the connection? He was obviously suspicious of Perry Long. But would he start to probe, ask awkward questions, and cause Cassie to doubt him, too? Even if Ben never found out that he was actually Arno Parson, he could still end up turning his role as Perry Long upside down. And that, too, would be very inconvenient, to say the least.

Then he saw his luck turn. Ben was not a man to sit on a rocker out on the porch and make polite conversation with someone he despised. It was not his cup of tea. Or mug of coffee, either.

"Cassie," he said, standing up. "Mr. Long. It's been my pleasure to see you. But I have pressing business. I must take my leave." And so, he did.

Seeing Ben get on his horse and ride away from Cassie's ranch, Martinez wrangled his motley crew in motion to follow the man. He was on the trail which led back to Joan's ranch. The gang kept hidden, and trailed him.

Once Ben was gone, Perry Long relaxed. He continued his flirting with the widow. He found he was trying too hard, because she was not responding as she had before Moss had come back on the scene. He knew Ben had been close with Cassie's dead husband. But he was ignorant of the true relationship between Cassie and Ben. What he did know was that Moss appeared concerned for her. He might have deeper feelings about her. Or not. Arno had not seen the kind of flirting between them that suggested anything more than friendship. Still, why did it seem

Cassie had started to cool on Perry Long, her gallant suitor, once Ben showed up?

Perry stayed, as invited, for dinner. Afterwards, he spoke quietly with Cassie out on the porch. He was looking ahead now. Tomorrow was key. The circuit judge would read the will and establish who would be trustee. One way or another, he would get his hands on that trust fund.

Then he'd be free to kill Ben Moss at his pleasure. He dropped a few vague hints, to give Cassie the idea his only concern was for Davis and his welfare. It was possible the judge might conclude it was in the boy's interest to name his uncle as trustee. But even if that happened, he told her, he wouldn't dream of removing Davis from his present living circumstance. The boy loved Cassie and her son and felt at home. That's how Perry wanted it, too. So he said.

Besides, Perry felt a duty to be a positive male influence on the boy. Davis hadn't had that. Perry thought it was high time he did.

So he suggested whichever one of them was named trustee, it seemed clear that the best outcome for Davis was for both of them to take charge of his welfare. Together. "And who knows where that could lead," he mused. "You're the kind of woman any man would be lucky to spend a lifetime with."

She didn't shoot it down. But she did say, "You're right, Perry. We don't know where all this is going to lead. So we should just take things one step at a time and think of Davis first."

With that, she said it was time to get some rest for the big day tomorrow. So Perry excused himself. Got into his fancy black buggy and said he looked forward to seeing her tomorrow for the reading of the will. As he drove off, he was frustrated that his seduction of the widow was proving harder than he had expected. But after tomorrow, and once he got his hands on the trust, the gloves could come off. Finally, he'd be in control. He'd settle all scores. And for once, he would stop feeling Harvey's judgment hanging over his head.

***

"Ben," Joan asked him in the morning, "do you have a decent change of clothes for today?"

"These are clean. Enough."

"For a sheep herder."

"Don't say that. This is Texas."

"Well, even folks in Texas dress respectable to show up in front of a judge. You ought to know that since you were a lawman."

"I ain't a sheriff now. And this ain't a trial."

"I will not have you appear before a judge looking like a saddle tramp."

"I don't plan to."

"Good. I'll dig up some decent clean clothes of Caleb's."

"No. What I'm saying is, I have no plan to go to the reading."

"What? But of course you will."

"For what?"

"For … all of us. Davis, and Cassie, and … her son." He noticed how she punched that last word. Staring at him like she'd caught him stealing the blueberry muffins.

"It's not my business."

"What about Slade? It's his business. He cares very much what happens to his best friend. I know you understand what that means."

"Do you really mean to bring Gary into this?"

"I don't know, Ben. Does that make you uneasy?"

"Why should it?"

Joan wanted to talk now—to get it all off her chest. The suspicion she'd clamped down on ever since her brother had disappeared. Since the wife of his dead friend had turned up pregnant. But ... she held her tongue again.

"If you don't care enough to make sure Cassie doesn't get swindled, then you can get back on that swayback, mule-eared, knock-kneed donkey you call a horse, and haul your ass back to New Mexico. Right now."

Joan had that look in her eye now. It hadn't changed since she was four years old and was as fierce as a rabid wolf. Besides, something nagged at Ben. It wasn't time yet to head back home. Too much unfinished business.

"All right, you old harpy. Fetch me some of Caleb's duds."

***

It didn't take five minutes for the Honorable Judge Foster Bass to read off the simple last will and testament of the late Martha Madden. The entire estate had been placed in trust, and Cassie Bohn was named as trustee.

"Before we proceed with a formal entry into the probate record, I would like to give anyone who has reason to step forward with any claim on this estate to do so." The judge pushed his reading glasses down on his nose, to peer over them for a look at the assembled citizens. One gentleman, dressed to the nines, was on his feet instantly.

"Your Honor," Perry Long began, his voice in a grave, low tone which he thought indicated respect and deference, "I would like to bring to your attention some information I feel is pertinent to this proceeding. If I may."

"Are you an attorney, sir?"

"I am not, sir."

"'Cause you look gussied up enough to pass for a slick city lawyer." The judge's comment brought suppressed chortles from all present, except for Ben. He guffawed out loud. Then clammed up again when people looked at him like a braying jackass. Which was just what he felt like.

Perry Long gave Ben a scathing look, then cleared his throat. "Your Honor. As most of her friends and neighbors know, Martha was not aware of any living relatives when she drew up her will." He glanced around, pleased no one contradicted him. "However, Martha was not correct. Because in fact, I am Perry Long, Martha's first cousin, on her mother's side."

"Interesting. Are you saying you make a claim of inheritance?"

"No indeed, sir. Not as such."

"Your point then?"

In far more words than necessary, Perry launched into a detailed, if rambling, tale of estranged family ties, foreign travels, and his heartbreak that his journey to reunite with his cousin had ended in the tragic circumstance that Martha had passed only days before he had reached Pendleton. Then he strained eloquence to filibuster His Honor with a lengthy sentimental recitation of his delight to discover his surviving nephew, Davis, and on and on and on …

Finally, Judge Bass cut him short. "Mr. Long. Notwithstanding your elucidating oratory on the piety of avuncular emotion, do you actually have a point to make?"

"The trusteeship, Your Honor. My point, sir, and I believe I am not alone in this sentiment, is that Martha completed her will in sound mind, but without the knowledge that she had any living relatives. It was no secret that on her deathbed, Marth confided to this lady," he gestured here at Cassie, "that she wanted Mrs. Bohn named trustee for the principal reason that there was no surviving relative to accept the duty. In ignorance, as she was, of yours truly."

"Mrs. Bohn? You're in concurrence with this purported set of facts?"

"I am, Your Honor. And so is Davis."

"Yes, sir," Davis piped up. "I was real glad meeting Uncle Perry, all right. It sure did lift my spirits."

"And are you, Mr. Long, as well as you, Mrs. Bohn, proposing to the court that we give consideration to whether Mr. Long should be considered as a co-trustee over this estate?"

"Yes, Your Honor," Perry snapped out as crisp as fried pork rinds.

"And have you any documentation to confirm your identity, sir?"

Perry felt the bottom drop. He looked at Cassie. And she piped up. "Your Honor, I have become acquainted with Mr. Long recently. He and Davis get along well, sir. And it might be good to have a masculine example present in the boy's life."

"I don't dispute that," Bass agreed. "He is welcome to be as much a presence in the boy's life as you all agree to. However … in order to make any formal alteration to the terms of the trusteeship, I would require firmer evidence. To establish his identity for the court, that is."

And then, a bright idea struck Cassie. "I think I can help there, sir." Perry sat up at this. *What's she talking about?* he wondered. "Before he came out this way, Mr. Long spent many years acquiring land rights for the railroad."

"Indeed? Which railroad did you work for, sir?"

"Sir? Uh … more than one, actually. Union Pacific, Southern Pacific—"

Judge Bass cut in, "Well, Mr. Long. Say no more. Speaking of cousins, my own cousin, Platt Bass, has been a vice president at Union Pacific for years. I'd be happy to show consideration for a U.P. man."

Perry's eyes lit up—he could almost feel the ill-gotten funds in his pocket now. "Sir, that is most understanding of you."

"Not at all, not at all. I shall just dash off a telegram to Platt at once and have him vouch for your identity." And he rapped a gavel down. "We shall reconvene on this matter at noon tomorrow."

CHAPTER TWELVE

As everyone filed out of the land office chambers, Ben noticed Davis and Slade were delighted. Cassie also looked pleased with the result—and her part in bringing it about.

But he noticed something else—Perry Long, or whoever this man was, was seething with anger. He made every effort to suppress it. And he did it well. Cassie and the boys didn't notice a thing. But Ben had been studying the face of Perry Long all this time. It was obvious that the man was lying. There never was any Perry Long who worked for the railroad. Or if there had been, the guy was probably dead in a ditch somewhere.

***

Perry Long's last buggy ride ferried Cassie, the boys, and himself out of Pendleton, headed for her ranch. As Ben watched them head out of town, Joan stepped in and began to scold him in a quiet tone. "Well. I might as well have stayed out of all this and kept my mouth shut."

"Aw, Joan. Nobody expected that," Ben said flatly. No smirk was visible.

"I mean, why did I bother to bring you at all? You didn't say a word. Just let him stand there and lie."

"And he didn't need any help doing that."

"So? You just aim to let him get away with it?"

"Oh, he won't."

"You're not all that convincing."

"Don't matter what I think. You, either. Judge Foster Bass will draw his own conclusions."

"Already has, it looked to me."

"Until he finds out Perry Long ain't who he claims. I saw the look on Long's face in there. He knows the jig's up. Wait and see."

***

As soon as the buggy pulled up, Slade and Davis leaped out. As they ran into the ranch house to peel off their fine duds, Cassie chuckled. "Look at 'em. Been clean far too long today. They'll have a lot of grubbing around to make up for."

She glanced over a Perry. Nothing. He wasn't even listening. Dark clouds boiled within him. "What's the matter?"

"Nothing."

"The judge sees things the same way we do. About what's good for Davis, I mean."

He turned to her. And when he willed his face to display a happy, positive expression, it appeared on command. "My dear, you are absolutely right. And as soon as those two Comanches head off on a buffalo hunt, or whatever, we ought to have a little celebration. Hmmm?"

Cassie looked at the upbeat expression Perry had on display. And she knew. Couldn't saw how, exactly. But there was something there, behind the eyes, that set off a warning. This man was not who she had believed he was. And as he followed Cassie into the house, a cold, uneasy feeling gripped her.

***

When Ben returned to the ranch with Joan and Caleb, he tried to push aside the prickle of wariness aside. As he casually swept his eyes over the surrounding wooded hills, he looked hard for a sign. He didn't see anyone. Not a hint of trouble. But as he dismounted Skip, he could tell the horse sensed something. A smell maybe. Or just some deep animal instinct. That twitchy unease that tells a prey animal to stay on alert. That something is watching.

Ben didn't plan to say anything about it. But as the sun got lower in the sky, he was determined to keep a watch that night. As he walked back to join Caleb and Joan in the ranch house, he ran his eyes over the tree line, scanning the ridges once more.

***

No sooner did the lads dash off, with Cassie's reminder to get back by dark, than she heard Perry over by the sideboard, pouring. He turned with a big smile and offered her a glass of amber liquid.

"This isn't the sherry, is it?"

Perry pulled a pint bottle of bonded rye from the inside pocket of his coat. "No, ma'am, it is not. Twelve-year-old bonded, best you can get. In these parts, anyway. Special, for a celebration."

"I see," she said politely, taking the glass. "Shouldn't we wait until the judge makes things official?"

He raised his glass. "To the mystery of creation." He quaffed the whiskey at a gulp. Raised his eyebrows to Cassie. She raised her glass, tipping it just enough to feel the touch of the rye against her lip. But she didn't actually swallow a drop. She put the glass down and started toward her bedroom. "Excuse me. I don't intend to make supper in my best dress."

"And you are a vision in whatever you wear." Or don't wear, he thought.

She walked past the flattery without comment, into her room. She closed the door behind her. She stopped for a moment, closed her eyes, and leaned back against the door. For some reason, she wished she could open it again to find that Perry Long had vanished. But that wasn't going to happen, and she knew it. She began to unfasten the buttons and remove her dress.

And then, behind her, the bedroom door swung open.

***

From his hidden vantage in the hills, Martinez had a perfect view of the yard in front of Joan's ranch house. What he could not see was the door to the root cellar, around the back. He did not know that a man who wanted to go down through the trapdoor in the kitchen floor could cross through, past the cool storage, and leave by those other cellar doors to the outside. Especially a man who could move as silently as Ben Moss.

***

"Get out!" Cassie shouted, so loudly that Perry Long stopped in his tracks. "How dare you?" she said, staying on the offensive. But she was trembling inside now. She knew it wouldn't be dark for at least half an hour. Until then, she was alone with this man, all on her own.

"Cassie, I'm sorry. My excitement got the better of me."

"Then get your excitement out of my room. Now."

He took a half step back, but did not move out the door. He held his hands up, trying to look open, peaceful, unthreatening—coming off as phony as that perfidious false face of his, pretending to be a grin. "I … Cassie, please listen. I've been bursting with this news all day."

"News? What news?"

"This," he said. And he drew a small box from his pocket. The stone in the ring he held out looked far too large to be real. "I can't wait a moment longer, Cassie. My feelings have grown too strong." She was shaking her head no. Hoping he would stop before he went too far. But he went right on ahead. "Ever since I set eyes on you, my passion has taken me prisoner. Now, the thought that we'll be sharing the responsibility for Davis, to raise him like a member of the family, if you will … Darling, nothing would make me happier than to consummate this union between us …"

"*Consummate?*" she sneered. "Isn't the word you mean '*consecrate*?'"

"Yes, exactly. Consecrate in holy matrimony. Tomorrow, by the hand of Judge Foster Bass. I ask you to join me in mind, in heart, and in flesh, as my wedded wife."

For a flicker of time, she let herself imagine what it would be like to become the wife of Perry Long. Gentleman, affectionate uncle, capable male role model for Davis. And for her own son. If that man she imagined were here, asking for her hand, she might just have said yes to his proposal.

But that man, that Perry Long, did not exist. The certainty of this took firm hold now. He could ape the role of a decent man, all right. He could sell it from now to Christmas. But she wasn't buying, not any more. His words were no better than the ring he was pushing. Not gold and diamond. It was brass and glass.

"I'm going to ask you just once more. Get out of my room."

But Perry Long was already gone. And now Arno Parson was the man pawing her with his black, greedy eyes. He took a step closer. "A woman like you, Cassie. You're not some dizzy bride. You understand the marriage bed. You know a man's needs. I expect you've learned your own desires, too. I expect you're just aching for it, after all this time." He took one more step.

Cassie responded. It was the answer to a question in the back of his mind all along. And that answer was yes. She did still carry a pistol concealed on her person. She knew how to cock it, and where to point it.

"Get. Out. Or. Else."

Arno didn't have a doubt she'd shoot him. Wasn't even sure she wouldn't shoot him in the back if he turned to run. He backed out, moving carefully through the door, and continued to step backwards through the parlor. Until he tripped over a tea kettle on a footstool.

He hit the ground at the same time the bedroom door slammed—and the front door banged open. Davis looked at him in puzzlement, blurting, "Uncle Perry?"

Slade was right behind him, calling "Ma? Is something wrong?"

Hearing the boys, and afraid of what this liar and cheat might do, Cassie opened the bedroom door again, keeping the pistol aimed. "He's just leaving, son. Say goodbye. He won't be back."

"What?" Davis blurted, a whine on the edge of his voice.

Arno Parson knew the game was over. His play was over, and he got to his feet and pushed Davis out of his way. "I ain't your damn uncle."

"Huh? I don't … what?"

"He's a liar, Davis," said Cassie. "I expect he was after the trust money all along."

Arno was almost out the front door, but he looked at Slade now. And hoping to spoon a little more hate into the stew, he said, "I ain't the only liar in this room, boy. Ask your father."

"You shut up. My father's dead."

"Maybe, maybe not. But he will be. That I can promise you."

And Arno Parson left. Perry Long was already long gone.

CHAPTER THIRTEEN

Arno used the whip liberally as the buggy raced away from Cassie's ranch. He was mad about the money, sure. Furious. But it was gone, over and done. He had to move on. That trust fund was just gravy. The meat of the plan was waiting for Arno at Caleb and Joan's ranch.

He ditched the buggy half a mile from Joan's place. He freed the horse, and rode it bareback up into the hills. Martinez heard him coming, crashing through branches and underbrush like he didn't care about anything. And when they all saw the murder in Arno's eyes, they knew plans had changed.

With the big payday gone, the only profit to be had from this goat grab would be to rustle the cattle off Joan's ranch. Kill Joan, kill Caleb, and most especially, kill Ben Moss once and for all. Then cut loose Cassie's herd, too, and pay her a final visit on their way out of the territory for good.

Arno led the gang down the wooded hill, toward the ranch house. When they reached the yard, he told Calby and Sammy Yost they should dash around back of the house to cut off any escape. The rest of the gang would attack the three trapped in the house from the front in a sudden rush. They would be all over them before Ben and his kin knew what was happening.

"All right, go!" Yost and Red Calby took off at a run, sprinting between the house and the barn. As soon as they rounded the corner, headed to the back of the house, Arno waved the rest to charge the front.

From the loft in the barn, Caleb had an open line of fire at three sides of the house—the front and yard, the side opposite the barn, and the back side. He took a bead on Red as he and Yost scurried toward the back. He held his fire until the other men charged toward the front of the house. Then he shot Red Calby in the spot just above the shoulder blades where the neck bone connected to the spine bone. Red Calby went down like a puppet with the strings cut.

Caleb's next shot knocked the hat off Sammy Yost's head, just a shade high, because the desperado was diving to hit the deck. While Yost desperately scrambled to find cover, Caleb hit him once in the thigh, then turned his rifle on the other five men and their frontal assault. Hitting Vern Ebersky seemed like shooting a buffalo with a bird gun. Three rapid hits slowed him down, but he was full of fight as he rolled behind a water trough for cover. By then Caleb had taken a bead on Jerry Quincy. His shot tore off Quincy's hat. But unlike Sammy Yost, along with his hat, Quincy was also minus the top half of his skull.

By this time, Ferd Martinez, who was quicker on the uptake than his brethren, figured out where the withering rifle fire was coming from. He got behind the pump for cover and started shooting at the barn. His first shot was wild, but he waited before taking a second shot. The loft opening was pitch-dark. But as soon as the man up there fired again, Martinez would shoot straight at the muzzle flash and take that gun out. He held his gun trained on the loft. He was truly surprised when the bullet fired from the wooded rise he had just left smashed two of his ribs and tumbled through his lungs, ripping terrible damage. It felt like being kicked by a mule, only with the hoof going right through him.

From his hiding place in the woods, Ben cocked the lever of the Winchester and put his next shot into Gandy's knee. Ben had gone out from the root cellar, and worked his way around behind the men hiding on the hill. As soon as they moved forward, he was right behind them. He took another shot at Gandy as he scrambled for cover, but didn't know if he got the knifeman.

The outlaws who were still alive all started to return wild fire in the general direction of the guns that now had them in a crossfire. They hit nothing.

Ben was trying to catch sight of the gang's leader—the man who had turned up just before ordering the assault. Perry Long. Who wasn't Perry Long. But whoever he was, he had managed to get himself out of sight.

Sammy Yost, by now, had slithered his way around the back of the house. Caleb could see him for an instant, fired, and missed. Yost tumbled down into the root cellar, wounded, but still armed and dangerous. He was under the house now. And inside the house, keeping her head down, was Joan.

Caleb didn't take even a second to consider what he must do. His job was to keep hidden, where he could fire down at the men below in the open, like shooting fish in a barrel. But that was before one of them got inside the house, where Joan was hiding. She did not even know the danger she was in.

Ben kept scanning the yard looking for Perry Long. He spotted the fat Polish butcher, trying to stay low behind the water trough. It offered shelter to Ebersky from any further gunfire out of the loft. Which was a waste, because Caleb was already down from the loft and starting his dash from the barn toward the house where his wife was in danger. Ebersky tried to rise just enough to get a shot at Caleb. From Ben's position, though, the water trough offered no protection. Before Ebersky could fire, Ben put three more slugs in him.

Ben couldn't see where Gandy was hiding. He knew the man was wounded, but was certain he was still dangerous. He could also see Martinez, lying in the yard by the pump. It was clear he wasn't dead yet. Because he was making ghastly, bubbling suck sounds, as he labored to get just a little air out of his torn up, blood-filled lungs. It was a race to see if he would drown in his own blood. But he was finished.

Now Ben heard Caleb, shouting as he ran out of the barn. "JOAN! There's one of them in the hou—" His warning was cut short as Martinez managed, with his dying breath, to squeeze the trigger one last time. Caleb went down hard.

Ben pumped lead into Martinez, firing again and again until his rifle was empty. *This was my fault*, his mind screamed. *Why didn't I finish him?* Ben dropped the empty rifle. He loosed his pistol and ran to where Caleb lay wounded. He found him gritting his teeth against the pain of a bullet wound that had entered just below the collarbone. He was bleeding profusely. Caleb also made the bleeding worse by trying to get back on his feet.

"Easy, easy," Ben said, as he ripped the sleeve off Caleb's shirt and tried to press it against the bleeding wound.

"Lemme go. Joan. That bastard's in the house!"

But Ben held him back. "I'll get him. Just stay down. Keep pressure on that." And Ben moved off quick, heading for the front door.

"Joan!" he called as he hurried toward the house. "Are you okay?"

Tripping on the porch step was the only reason Gandy's throwing dagger missed Ben and stuck into the wooden door instead. Gandy came like smoke from the shadows, Bowie knife already arcing toward Ben. That blade hammered into the wooden porch an inch from Ben's head at the same time he fired his pistol into the knifeman's belly. It did not keep Gandy from flicking some catch that sent a spring-loaded switch blade from the sleeve on his wrist into his hand. He was on top of Ben, trying with all his strength and weight to drive the dagger blade down into Ben's face. For a smaller man, Gandy had incredible upper-body strength, and Ben's arms trembled with the effort of trying to keep the blade away. But with his body weight behind him, Gandy was slowly grinding down, down, almost close enough to break the skin.

But Ben could feel the hot, wet blood flowing freely out from Gandy's gunshot wound. As the lifeblood left his body, so did his strength. Gandy gradually began to lose the battle, and Ben was pushing the knife away from his face, inch by inch. Then Gandy's grip weakened, and Ben knocked the knife away. He rolled, flipping Gandy off him. Now Gandy was on his back, and the entire front of him was awash in gore. His hand trembled as it seemed to crawl on its own will, moving over his chest, and trying to pull another knife out of a hidden breast pocket. It was almost clear of his vest when Gandy went still, the light in his eyes going dark.

Ben jumped up and kicked in the front door, pistol ready. He heard a sound in the kitchen—a squeaking hinge. He knew the sound—it was the one he'd heard when he opened that trapdoor to the cellar. It must be Yost, coming up from the root cellar. Ben moved fast, bounding the five steps that took him to the kitchen to face Yost.

Only Yost suddenly had no face. Joan, in a chair by the kitchen table, cut loose with the Browning shotgun as soon as Yost stuck his head up from the cellar, and nearly decapitated him.

And that was it. The seven men in the gang that served Perry Long were all dead. The only man missing was their leader. It made sense to Ben now. He had known, the moment he saw Perry Long turn up and start giving orders. These were the ruffians who had molested Cassie. And Perry Long had put them up to it, just to set himself up as Cassie's savior. Perry Long. A gang of rustlers. That familiar face … Could it be? He tried to picture the slick dandy with a bushy black beard. Imagined that pomaded hair with its sharp crease of a part down the middle being eight inches longer, and hanging like a greasy curtain around his face. He recognized that face at last. Arno Parson.

Ben and Joan dashed back outside. Caleb was pale, but the bleeding had slowed. "There's a bullet in there. Gotta come out, now."

Joan was looking around the yard in a daze. "My God … you … killed them all..."

"Not all of them. Parson got away."

"Wha— Parson? Are you sure?"

Caleb gripped Ben's arm. He had just one thought. "Cassie."

"We need to get you to Doc Ensel," Ben said.

"I can get him into the buckboard. You get after that outlaw."

"She's right," Caleb said. "I'll make it. Go."

CHAPTER FOURTEEN

Arno Parson looked like hell. The knees of his trousers were torn. His fine leather shoes were caked with mud. The derby was gone; there was nothing to hide the bloody gash on his scalp. Blood dripped from his head and left dime-sized dots of red on his starched white collar. The sleeve of his jacket had a torn seam at the shoulder. And he smelled; the rank, sour stink of flop-sweat and fear.

Cassie's house was dark when he arrived. Good. At least he had time to rinse some of the blood off. He didn't count on the scream of squeaky iron when he started to pump water, but he didn't care. It felt good to let the cool water run over his overheated, bloody head.

Cassie wasn't asleep anyway. At the first squeal of that pump handle, she was out of her room and waking the boys. One peek told her that the slimy rascal was back again. She shushed the boys. Opened their window. Told them to go to Joan's and fetch Ben. No questions, do it! They were out and off into the darkness when the knock came on her door.

"Get off my land," she said.

"Open that door or I'll break it down."

Cassie pulled the trigger, and her .45 caliber answer punched through the door and just missed Arno Parson. He hopped down off the porch and took out his gun. He put a slug of his own through the door, though he hoped it would not hit Cassie, only scare some sense into her.

"Let me in. We have business that isn't finished yet."

"No. We're finished. But if you want to dispute that, try opening that door."

"You don't want to start any gunplay. Someone might get hurt."

"It won't be me."

"But you're not alone. It might be one of your boys." He let that settle, expecting it to worry her badly. "I don't even have to come in. I can just set your place on fire."

"And I'm telling you to get. The boys aren't here."

"I don't believe you. Where would they go in the middle of the night?"

"Straight to Joan's. To fetch Ben and Caleb. And if you're still here, God help you."

***

Slade and Davis had sprinted to the corral to jump on their horses. But when they heard that first gunshot, Slade stopped. "Go on, Davis. I ain't leaving Ma alone."

"Well, I ain't either," he whispered fiercely.

"Somebody has to get Ben."

"I'm the oldest. You do it."

"I ain't leaving."

"Me neither."

They glared stubbornly at each other. Finally, Slade said, "Fine. Then let's get that squirrel rifle out from the barn."

"Now you're talking," Davis agreed. And they ran to the barn.

***

"The harder you make this, the rougher it's gonna be on you."

"Open that door, and we'll find out."

Arno was grinding his teeth in frustration. She'd messed this up. Had to open her big mouth to the judge. Why the hell did he ever make up that stupid story about being some bigshot on the railroad? That was her fault, too. Acting all high and mighty. Making him feel the need to boast. To make himself bigger. Well, he was going to teach her a lesson. And he meant to enjoy it, too.

That was when he heard a noise over by the barn.

***

Davis pulled the squirrel rifle down off the pegs in the barn wall.

"Give it here," Slade said.

"Not a chance. Where's the ammo?"

Slade felt a shameful blush rush through him. "Damn."

"What're you cursing for?"

"Them bullets are in my room."

"Ain't that just perfect."

"I wasn't planning on shooting anybody's uncle tonight, okay?"

"Well, he ain't my uncle. So I'll shoot him."

"What with?"

They both pondered this for a moment. Davis got a notion. "He don't know if it's loaded or not. "I'll point it right in his face. See if he don't give up."

"That's stupid."

"I ain't scared of him."

"Listen, you hold off. I can run back, sneak in the window, and get back here with the bullets. Then we both get him."

"No. I'll go with you. Then we'll plug him."

The two boys started to creep out of the barn. Davis was leading, holding the squirrel gun. As soon as the barrel of the rifle poked out the door of the barn, Arno seized the barrel and yanked Davis out, tripping him. Before Slade could do anything, he was looking at the pistol Arno had trained on him.

"No tricks. Hands up. Let's go." And he began marching his prisoners over to the ranch house.

***

Cassie took a moment to wipe the sweat off her brow with her sleeve. It didn't stop her from sweating, though. She felt a single trickle roll down her side, from her armpit, all the way down to her waist, under the nightshirt she had on. What was he up to? He wouldn't really set the house afire. Would he? But then she remembered hearing about how railroad thugs burned a whole family alive in their house, when they wouldn't sell and clear out.

Then she heard something more frightening than the strike of a match. It was the voice of her son, Slade, trying so hard not to cry. "Ma? He says you better open the door."

"I want to hear you drop that gun first. Mine's pointed right at your son's heart. I'm all out of patience."

"Slade? Are you okay?"

Davis was still stung with the shame of getting the rifle taken. "Don't do it, Cass—" and before he finished, Arno slammed the barrel of the gun on his head. Davis dropped to the porch with a crash. Out cold.

"What happened? What was that?"

"Just a taste of what's coming for these two, if you don't drop that gun and open the door."

"You promise not to hurt them?"

"I can promise I will, at the count of three … One …"

"Davis? Did he hurt you?"

"He hit him on the head, Ma." Then Cassie heard the slap of a hand, and Slade yelped as the open palm smacked his cheek.

"Slade!"

"Two …"

The chunky thump of the gun hitting the floor made Arno smile. "That's the right choice, Cassie. Now, open the door."

As the door swung open, Arno shoved Slade in ahead of him, hard. The boy stumbled, and almost fell, but Cassie caught him. Beyond Arno in the doorway, she could see Davis, sprawled and lifeless.

"Don't fret about him," Arno said. "He'll wake up with a headache, is all."

"That must make you feel like a big man."

"Oh, sweetheart, I'm just getting that part started." He looked across the parlor, toward the boys' bedroom. There was a keyhole on the lock plate. "Son, fetch the key for that door."

Arno gave Slade a push to get him going. He got the key off a nail on the wall. Arno then shoved him into the bedroom, shut the door, and locked it. "Boy? Come out of there, right now." He heard Slade try the knob, trying to turn it. It rattled a little, but the door wouldn't budge.

"Good. You can have a little privacy." His leering face showed growing excitement. He grabbed Cassie by the arm and dragged her toward her bedroom, as he added, "And so can we, darlin'." He let go of her arm and took a handful of her bottom, squeezing tight as he steered her into the bedroom.

***

Ben arrived at the Bohn ranch and felt a cold fury seize his gut as he spotted Davis, lying unconscious. Ben drew his gun, creeping silently to the porch. He could feel a strong pulse when he felt the boy's neck. Alive, at least.

Then he heard a short cry of pain from Cassie, followed by a slap. "You're gonna take that off now. Or I may have a go at your boy first."

"I'm sure that's your style. Parson."

Arno's smile lit up his face like Christmas. It was all how he wanted it now. It was perfect. He dug his fingers into Cassie's hair and twisted her sharply around in front of him, blocking Ben's shot.

"Finally figured it out, huh, sheriff?"

"Skunk's a skunk, no matter how much cologne you pour on it."

"How pithy. Now, let me tell you how this goes." Arno pulled out a set of handcuffs. "Step out onto the porch."

At gunpoint, he marched Ben to the support post for the porch roof which was nearest the front door. He cuffed Ben with his hands behind him and his arms around the post, so he was facing the house. "Good, good," he said. "A nice open view into the parlor. And the couch. Oh, you'll get to watch everything from here."

"Too bad about all that money," Ben said.

Arno batted him across the jaw with the butt of his pistol. Ben spit blood in his face, and Arno almost lost control. But he didn't.

"I know you'd like me to kill you now and get it over with. But you are going to pay for killing my brother. First, you are going to watch me defile the mother of your son. Oh yes. You may have taken your time figuring out who I am. But I only needed one look to know you and the widow did that deed."

Ben looked at Cassie, who was crying. He knew that she'd done her best to keep the truth from everyone. Even him. But Arno was right. Slade was his own son.

"Then you and Ma can watch me cut that boy into strips of jerky. Then it's Cassie's turn. Then you, taking it slow as can be."

Ben was straining to test the support beam. It seemed impossible to break free.

"Oh, but I almost forgot. Do you know why I want you to suffer so much for killing my brother?" Arno pointed at the unconscious body of Davis. "And why killing you will not just be revenge for me, but for Davis here? Because when you rode Harvey down and shot him like a dog—you killed an innocent man. Harvey isn't the one who shot your friend, Gary. I did. I killed him right there, while Harvey was trying to stop the fight and make a truce. Now, Harvey had his faults. But his real crime is, he betrayed me. And all our gang, too. But I was his brother. I looked up to him as a leader. And he let me down. He tried to walk away. Act all high and mighty 'cause he married a woman who could support him. He wouldn't ride with us, but he didn't let us free. Never said, 'Arno, my brother, these are your men now. You're the real leader of the Parson gang.'"

Arno spat in disgust. "But once I came here, to this crappy patch of dirt, and rustled them cows and shot that sodbuster dead? Well, Harvey had no choice. He had to ride with us. And never look back at this cowpat of a town again. Back with the Parson gang, where he belonged. Only that didn't happen. Because you killed him. So, what you see next, what you have to watch me do to your woman, and your son, maybe you'll know how I felt watching you ride my brother down and kill him."

Ben hung his head. He had killed the wrong Parson. It was Arno all along. He was the one who had pushed over the whole house of cards.

"Now then," said Arno, cracking his knuckles and starting to remove his glossy black hand-tooled belt. "Time for the fun to begin. You have a good enough view here? Or should I drag Cassie right out here on the porch, so you can have a better look? Your call, Ben."

Ben had nothing he could do except spit in Arno's face again. This time, when the spit hit him, Arno couldn't hold off. He rapped the gun barrel across Ben's face again. Then he stopped, as inspiration struck.

"Just a sec. I thought of something. All I need healthy is your eyes so you can see the fun. But you can still see without fingers. Hell, I can start on them now. Blow them off one at a time. Yeah, that's a good idea." Arno stepped off the porch and got behind Ben, looking to see if he had a clear shot at his hands, manacled as they were behind him.

"Let's see now. Start on the pinky? Or go for the thumbs first?" Ben heard the hammer of Arno's gun cock. "Eeny-meeny-miney-mo. When I get done with the fingers, I'll still have your—"

The report of the squirrel gun sounded like a tiny pop. The small .22 caliber round hit Arno about half an inch above his ear. Little tiny hole. But the high velocity of a small round was what did the real damage, tumbling through brain tissue, bouncing off the inside of the skull, and ripping apart the rest of Arno Parson's brain.

Ben turned his head. Slade was standing by the corner of the house, holding the rifle. He worked the bolt, and the little brass casing ejected. He bent down and put it in his pocket, just like Uncle Caleb had always taught him to do. The locked door hadn't stopped him from going back out the window and finding that squirrel gun.

"Mighty fine shot, son."

"Thank you, sir … I mean … Dad."

EPILOGUE

Edgar Latham felt his heart soar as he watched the wagon coming from the East, swaying and clattering, drawing closer. It was stuffed with everything Cassie could pack into it.

She'd still left a lot of stuff behind, back in Texas. She had given anything she couldn't carry on that big Conestoga to Joan. Her new sister-in-law.

And the best sight Edgar Latham had for enjoyment was seeing Ben, with a long, thin switch in his hand, urging the oxen along.

Ben the oxherd. Ben, the married man. Married to a woman he had always loved.

It sounded delicious as he rolled it around on his tongue. It would be a wonderful thing to tease Ben about. It would be a treasure for many years.

Right now, Edgar Latham was also feeling rather more elevated in his station in life. He saw the two boys coming to live here with Cassie and Ben on the ranch as a good thing. He knew, with the proper guidance, he could shape these two into men who were real, professional cowboys. Men who could do whatever was necessary. Men with the skill to make the ranch even more successful than it already was.

And why shouldn't it be? After all, the ranch foreman who ran things was the best boss a cowhand could ever have.

And Cassie and Slade were the best things that had ever happened to Ben. He was sure of it.

The End